"*Nothing's Ever The ...* ... ...eet snapshot of a fami... ... be-lievable voice I've ... ...nal tone is as straightf... ...r a knife to the heart."

> — **Rob Rufus, ALA Award-winning author of *Die Young With Me***

"A heartfelt and bittersweet tale, told with the sort of insight and eloquence we've come to expect from the fiction of Cyn Vargas. A master of the 'child dealing with the problematic behavior of adults' short story, this time Cyn gives us a novella-length tale with a teen-girl hero you can't help but root for, the paradise of a childhood innocence lost, and something like the beginning of mature understanding gained. A most satisfying read, to be sure."

> — **Eric Charles May, author of *Bedrock Faith***

Nothing's Ever the Same

"With a keen sense of observation and a sharp sense of humor, Cyn Vargas fully inhabits the voice of Itzel, the narrator of *Nothing's Ever the Same*. A moving story of family and the ways we hurt and survive one another, *Nothing's Ever the Same* is like Itzel herself: smart, funny, poignant, and real. With this heartfelt novella, Cyn Vargas reminds readers once again why she was named "A Writer to Watch" by Chicago's Guild Literary Complex. Watch her; read her."

> — **Patricia Ann McNair, author of *Responsible Adults***

Nothing's Ever The Same

Nothing's Ever The Same

A Novella

Cyn Vargas

Tortoise Books
Chicago

FIRST EDITION, MAY, 2024
Copyright © 2024 by Cyn Vargas

Published in the United States by Tortoise Books
www.tortoisebooks.com

ASIN: B0CHDVKYC9
ISBN-13: 978-1-948954-87-7

Cover Design: Gerald Brennan

Tortoise Books Logo Copyright ©2024 by Tortoise Books.
Original artwork by Rachele O'Hare.

To Mom,

Thank you for always believing in me, loving me entirely, and texting me random emojis every morning. This book is dedicated to you with all my love and gratitude.

Angioplasty & Piñatas

The first time I saw my mom cry was after my dad's heart attack. I was thirteen and on the swing set that was left behind by the people that owned the house before. I never had a swing set that was mine nor a house that was mine, and this was going to be the first birthday party I had in a backyard that was ours.

I swung so high in the long purple dress that Mom saved up all month to buy me, and saw Dad trying to tie the rope of the piñata around the gutter of my second-floor bedroom window. Our neighbor, Don Julio, stood on a ladder tying the other end of the rope around a branch of the only tree in our yard. It was skinny and tall like Olive Oyl.

"I had it made just for you," Dad said. The piñata, in shape of a huge 13 covered in orange, blue, and yellow paper strips, swayed in the fall breeze. Before that, Dad had always gotten me small piñatas because we'd lived in an apartment. Back then the piñatas were miniature unicorns, birds, even that Trix Rabbit on TV. Each year, one hung off the broken ceiling fan in the living room. We used a spatula taped to the end of the broom to hit it and after a few good whacks, Dad ripped it open with his hands like King Kong. Candy flying everywhere.

That landlord wouldn't let us use the backyard cause he didn't want his grass to get mashed up. I think he meant messed up, but I didn't correct him cause his lazy eye gave me the creeps. He had at least fifteen different-sized *Do Not Walk On Lawn* signs scattered around the yard. The sticks from them made so many holes they ruined the grass.

But after moving into the house, Dad got me the biggest piñata he could. "To make up for all the years they were the size of beans," he said.

Now Dad and Don Julio kept yelling back to one another.

"Pull the rope up higher on your side!"

"No, lower!"

The piñata dancing there in mid-air.

Mom set up the two tables outside with yellow plastic covers.

"Leo! Be careful! You're going to fall and kill yourself!"

"Let me be, woman, or I will!"

Cumbias and the scent of tamales lingered from the open kitchen window. Each time my swing went down and back, I saw my cake on the kitchen table. It was rectangular, covered in white frosting. *Itzel* spelled out in purple frosting surrounded by candles and colorful plastic balloons.

"That's way too high!" I heard and that could've been for me. I swung so high; my new white shoes almost scraped the back of a pigeon. The sky started to move further and further away from me when I heard screams.

I saw Mom looking at the house. She had been pouring orange soda into Styrofoam cups but now the liter fell open on the table. Orange soda blots on her ivory pants. The swing was still going so fast. I caught a glimpse of Dad's hand in the window. Just one hand and then it was gone. Mom rushed into the house. Don Julio jumped off the ladder and ran towards the house too.

Planting my feet onto the grass, I forced the swing to slow down way too fast. The momentum threw me onto the ground and I fell on my knees hard. I was sure one was bleeding, but I didn't check. I ran into the house. Don Julio was on the phone in the kitchen giving the person on the other side my address. I ran up the stairs to my room. Dad was on the floor not moving. Mom was over him giving him CPR, pushing on his chest and blowing air into his mouth. His arms on his sides, palms up, silent. Mom never looked at me and I never looked away. I stood and watched from the doorway. I wanted to run over and hug Dad. I wanted Mom to hug me, but I couldn't move. My room was the size of a cigar box, but they seemed so far away. She didn't stop CPR until the ambulance came. Don Julio followed the paramedics into the room.

There were two of them. Both seemed surprised Mom knew CPR. They shrugged their shoulders to one another.

"She's a nurse," I said, but I wasn't sure they heard me.

One took over for Mom, so she moved next to me and clenched my hand. It was cold and I wasn't sure if it was because she was scared or because it was cold from Dad.

"Let's go downstairs," Don Julio said to me.

But Mom didn't budge. She stared at Dad and the two strangers trying to save him.

"I'm not going unless my mom does."

Mom's pink lipstick was smeared across one cheek. Her eyes glossed over. She nodded.

Don Julio went through the narrow doorway first. We followed him. I looked back, but Mom was behind me and I couldn't see anything.

"I'm going to go get Sylvia. She can stay here while I take you to the hospital," Don Julio ran out the door to get his wife.

Mom's hand quivered as she turned off the stove. The water stopped boiling. The wind shook the open window frame. I peered outside at the swirling red and white lights. The table covers were nowhere to be seen.

Mom was trained to be calm. I was not. I cried so hard; I couldn't catch my breath. She brought me in to her. My head on her chest. Her apron smelled of sweet corn.

"Your dad will be fine," she said, but I wasn't sure she believed it.

The paramedics came down with Dad on a stretcher. I hadn't even seen them bring it in.

"He's stable for now. You can meet us at the hospital."

They carried him through the kitchen. His face covered with an oxygen mask. He still wasn't moving.

Doña Sylvia and Don Julio rushed in as the ambulance took off. "Go on, Don Julio. I'll let people know what happened."

I jumped into the backseat of Don Julio's car and saw a yellow tablecloth caught in some weeds across the street. The ride to the hospital seemed so long. Mom was silent except for the house keys she fiddled with. Don Julio exhaled every ten seconds, his head shifting from side to side to see the traffic ahead. Every light was red. Stop signs popped up that I'd never seen before. Every car in front of us dawdled. The hospital wasn't far, but it might as well have been in the next time zone. By the time I felt a scream coming on, we had finally arrived.

The hospital was so shiny. I was nearly blinded when we rushed into the emergency room. Everyone seemed to be moving fast, but not in a rush. Don Julio and I sat down in the waiting room while Mom went to speak to the front desk lady.

"They are taking him into surgery," Mom told us. "Don Julio, thanks so much for everything. Please. Go on back. Sylvia must be overwhelmed over the way I left the house."

"But Doña Luna—"

"Please Don Julio. He'll be in surgery for hours. I'll call you if anything. I promise."

Don Julio stood and shook her hand, "Don Leonardo is a great man. God will bless him. I will pray for him."

I wanted to ask him why God didn't bless my dad in the first place.

Once Don Julio left, Mom took my hand and said, "We have nothing left to do." I thought she was going to add *except to pray* like she did many times before when things happened, but she didn't say it this time.

She started to cry. Her elbows on her knees, her face buried into her hands. I had never seen her cry before. I then started to cry too. And we just sat there next to each other. Only stopping after a long time.

We barely talked for the next few hours except when she asked if I wanted something from the vending machines. I shook my head. I didn't want to go alone and I didn't want her to come with me in case the doctor came back. So I just held her hand and put my head on her arm. I thought of Dad and the funny way he could never get his pancakes to come out round.

I woke up to a woman in a white coat mid-sentence with Mom. "—angioplasty. He should be ready to go home in the next couple of days. He'll have to change his diet and increase his physical activity. You can see him early tomorrow. You two go home and get some rest."

Mom called a cab. We never took cabs and I wasn't sure if it would be all cloudy with cigarette smoke and have slippery green seats with silver duct tape covering up the rips like the cabs on TV. The one we got into didn't have one piece of tape anywhere on it and instead had polished green leather seats and smelled like pine trees.

"I don't understand what angioplasty means," I said.

"That means they put a balloon in the arteries of his heart."

And I imagined a small plastic birthday balloon in Dad's chest.

The Other Side

Dad was back home two days later. The house still smelled like tamales. Don Julio's side of the rope was still hanging off of the branch. The piñata was now colorful thin mush because it had rained while Dad was away. Deformed egg-shaped candy inside the wet cardboard.

Mom had waited to tell Tia Amelia about Dad until she saw her in person. After what happened to Tio Bernardo and the primos, there was no way Tia Amelia could handle any phone call that had the words *emergency* or *hospital* in it even if *but he's OK* came after.

Dad sat on his favorite recliner, covered up to his waist in this gray blanket he got for free after twenty car washes. He drank tea. Dad didn't like tea.

"You need something, Dad?"

"Come over here, Itzel," He waved me over. The TV was on, but on mute. It was some old Western movie with a few horses that I figured were long since dead. Then again I didn't really know how long horses lived.

"I haven't told your mom this, so don't tell her."

He paused until I agreed to not tell Mom anything.

"I went to the other side."

"The other side of what?" I was about to joke and say, *the other side of the road?* because Dad would've said that if it was the other way around, but he wasn't laughing. He wasn't even blinking. So instead, I just nodded again and sat on the arm of the recliner.

"I'm not sure how long it was. Maybe a few seconds or minutes. There was no time really. I remember hanging your piñata and looking at your mom. The wooden spoon and fork pattern on her apron matched the yellow covers she was putting on the tables. I remember thinking how beautiful she looked there in her own home. Finally, her own house.

Then...I don't know. I didn't feel anything. It was just black, like floating in space without the stars. There were no heavenly angels and golden clouds, and no little devils with black eyes and sharp teeth. There was nothing, Itzel. Nothing. It was how it was."

Dad talking about being in some empty black space without angels or scary demons wouldn't leave my head. He said there was nothing. He was in nothing, and that's not what Father Joe said in church. If you are good, you go to heaven and if you are bad, you go to hell.

A couple years before we moved into the house, my Tio Bernardo and primos died. Mom said they were in heaven, but I wasn't sure why God would need them in heaven so soon. I didn't know how old Tio Bernardo was, but he wasn't a viejito and Memo and Neno were only three.

Mom and Dad just told me there was a car accident. But at the funeral, I heard people talking. Some whispered when they saw me or other kids walk by, but others sounded like they were talking through one of those megaphones the principal used to get us inside school after recess.

Tio Bernardo was wearing his seatbelt. My primos were in their car seats. A big blue truck smashed into Tio Bernardo's car. All of them died right away. Tia Amelia screamed so loud then fainted. *They all went to heaven.* That's what everyone kept saying, but what if they were where Dad said he had been? What if they were in nothing?

I jumped when the alarm clock went off.

"Let me get your pills, Dad," I didn't really look at him as I went into the kitchen.

Mom had put all the pill bottles on the counter next to the toaster. Each one had a piece of paper under it with the neatest, largest writing she had ever used. *1:00 pm*, one said. *3:30 pm WITH FOOD*, said the other. There were a couple more and I spotted the one that he had to take.

"Here Dad," I tried to give him a glass of water and the pill. He instead folded his hands on his lap and closed his eyes.

"C'mon Dad."

"I'm sleeping."

"Dad."

"A sleeping person can't take a pill. They'll choke."

"Sure, Dad. You really look like you're sleeping."

He opened his eyes and laughed. Dad was finally Dad again. We never spoke about the other side again.

Los Abuelos & The White Quilt

I was closest to my Abuelita Rosa. She'd pick me up from school and pay for candy at the corner store from money she took out of her bra. She had a purse with a wallet inside, but said, *that is too obvious for the thieves. Let them run with my bag. Trick them,* and then she'd pat her breast like she was gently trying to wake it up from a nap. I didn't want to get robbed, but I wasn't too worried about it. I didn't need a purse, wallet, or bra. I didn't have any money or boobs.

For my communion, Abuelita helped me put on my dress. Mom had run to the market to get the cake for afterwards. Dad was helping Abuelito put on his tie.

"I had this dress made just for you. The best seamstresses are in Guatemala City. Look how beautiful it is."

I looked at myself in the full-size mirror she had on the back of her closet door. The dress was clouds stitched together. Sprinkles of pearls along the seams of the sleeves and the waist and in twirls around the bottom like glass petals.

"Thanks, Abuelita," and I meant it. Not like when she bought me a winter hat the year before that had bunny ears that went past my shoulders. I couldn't wear that to school, but I said thank you because she was my abuelita and she always thought of me.

Abuelita also showed me how to make a quilt. On Sunday afternoons, I'd go over to my abuelos' house and Abuela and I would work on the quilt together.

"Coffee for the señoritas?" Abuelo always asked us. Abuela nodded every time and so did I. Mom and Dad wouldn't let me have coffee back home. They said it would make me shorter than I already was. Abuelo would bring us each a cup of coffee. Mine mostly milk. He then sat on the couch and took a nap sitting up for the next two hours. Abuela and I sipped our coffee, making sure not to get any on the quilt.

Way Up There

When I was eight, a neighborhood kid was riding her bike while I sat on the handlebars with my arms up in the air. The girl was going faster and faster until *boom*. She hit a bump and next thing I know I smashed face-first into the sidewalk. My pink glasses broke in two perfect pieces. Blood poured out of my nose. My face was on fire. When Mom opened the door to the neighborhood girl crying and holding my hand, it was the first time I heard her swear in English.

I sat on the toilet. Mom was standing over me holding the new white bath towel against my face.

"Your nose is fine, thank God," she said, though when she washed off the blood and stood back to look at my nose, she tilted her head from one side to the other.

I knew something wasn't right. I stood up and looked in the mirror. Without my glasses, I had to hold onto the sink, go on my tiptoes and lean forward for the blurs to straighten out. There I was. My bangs tangled within themselves; some strands stuck to the side of my face with dry tears. A scratch on my forehead as thin as thread. I was wrong about the blood coming from my nose. My nose was fine. My mouth and lips were fine. The groove between my nose and my lips was not fine.

There was a tiny hole there. I saw my flesh. I saw blood, though it was starting to dry. I never had a hole in my face that didn't belong.

"Do I need to go to the doctor?"

"No. It'll heal just fine. You'll see," and she kissed my forehead, being careful not to kiss the scratch. She put that liquid brown medicine on the gash under my nose. It stung and sizzled. Mom then gave me some gross red medicine to drink for the pain.

It was a Sunday and los abuelos came over for dinner. Abuela came into my room. My head throbbing from all the crying.

"Don't tell my mom, ok? But I'm ugly." I started to cry again.

"You aren't ugly, Itzel. You know what I hear helps speed the healing?" and she took out a bar of Hershey's chocolate. She un-wrapped half of it and then broke off a square and gave it to me. She was right. It did make me feel better.

Even after I healed, Abuela and I would share Hershey's chocolate before dinner on Sunday nights.

Rosary & The Why

A month after Dad had the heart attack, Abuela Rosa had something wrong with her, too. They called it a stroke. She didn't wake up though like Dad did. Back in the hospital we went. Back to the shiny floors that reflected the ceiling tiles with pockmarks. All the doctors in white, all the nurses in pastel colors. The beeps and the people calling doctors over the intercom and the screech of the chairs against the tile every time someone shifted in their seat.

I wasn't allowed to see Abuela for three days. She was in intensive care and only Abuelo, Mom and Tia Amelia could see her. Dad stayed with me while we waited for Mom.

"Did I ever tell you what your grand-mother told me when I asked your mom to marry me?"

I searched for more Cheetos in my bag, but the ones that came out of the vending machines always seemed to have no more than seven in them. I shook my head.

"Doña Rosa said, 'If you break her heart, I'll break your balls.'"

I stopped with the Cheetos bag and stared at Dad.

"Yup, your sweet grandma," he chuckled. "She's a kind woman, but she also doesn't take any crap, especially when it came to your mom or Amelia. I had just asked your mom to marry me and she was so happy even with the little ring I gave her. It was all I could afford. 'Mom, look!' she said when we walked back into the house. Luna held her hand up high and stared at the ring as she walked instead of straight ahead, but it was her house, so she could have walked through there with her eyes closed.

"Your grandma put down the spoon she was using to mix whatever she was cooking. All I can remember is that it smelled delicious and I was so hungry. I had been saving up money for the ring, so all I ate were peanut butter sandwiches and let me tell you, after a couple of months of that, you forget what real food tastes like."

"Is that why you don't like PB&J sandwiches?" Thinking about it, I'd never seen him eat one in my whole life.

"You got it, Itzel. So, Doña Rosa puts the spoon down and looks at the ring and Luna's big smile and my big smile and she smiles and says, *'I'm so happy for you two. Wait till your dad wakes up. We'll tell him over dinner!'* and Luna says, *'I can't wait, Mama!'* and runs upstairs to tell her dad. So, there is your grandma and me in the most territorial room of her house—the kitchen. She was always nice to me, especially since she knew that my parents had died when I was very young. She took me in as family. Anyway, she says, *'Leonardo. I know how much you love my daughter and I know how much she loves you. I bless your marriage,'* and she smiles. So, I go to hug her and she says, *'One moment, please.'* She turns around, swirls the food in the pan, and turns back with the wooden spoon in her hand and points at me with it. I could see the smoke off the top of it. *'I say this with much love in my heart.'* And I thought she was going to tell me I should've gotten her blessing first, but she says, *'If you break her heart. I break your balls.'* And I thought she was joking because she never even said the word *damn*, so I laughed. Doña Rosa did not laugh. I nodded. She nodded and then smiled and hugged me. Your mom walked in on that and cried happy tears, as they say."

Abuela never swore or ever really got angry except when Tia Amelia's family died. One of the many nights the whole family came over and prayed the rosary, I sat next to Abuela and she whispered, *Why would God do this?* She was angry. At God. Abuela never missed church. Knew which sacrament was in what order. If getting a tattoo wasn't against the Catholic religion, she'd probably have had all fourteen

Stations of the Cross inked across her back. I'd never heard her sound angry at God before. *God knows what He does and why.* That's what she said whenever something good *or* bad happened, but she wasn't saying that now.

I'm mad too, I wanted to tell her. I didn't understand. Why did God take away my Tio and my primos? What did they ever do to Him? Mom and Dad weren't big on church. Was He going to kill us too?

I moved the rosary through my hands without paying attention to what we were supposed to say. I heard Abuela say, *Forgive me, Lord.* She was crying. I wasn't sure if she was crying because she felt bad or because she was still angry. Or both.

I was about to ask Dad if he ever told Mom what Abuela said, but that's when Mom came through the waiting room door.

"Leo, they are sending her to hospice," The last words barely came out and she started to bawl. Dad got up and held her. I didn't know what hospice was, but whatever it was, I didn't want Abuela to go there.

Heart Is Home

We walked into a room where families were eating at round tables and a TV showed some kid falling off the playground and cutting his face. The kid starts to cry and what looked like his dad jumps off the bench and carries him running towards somewhere. The TV was on mute and the closed captioning was giving me a headache. All I read was *"Billy!"* before I turned away.

Tia Amelia and Abuelo were sitting at the table. Fruit and sandwiches in front of them, untouched.

"The doctor is checking in on her and asked us to wait out here," Abuelo said to no one in particular. Mom nodded. Dad sat down next to him and put the cup of coffee that was in front of him closer to Abuelo. Abuelo wrapped his hands around it and nodded, but he didn't take a sip.

"You can see her now," a nurse strolled up to the table and smiled. Mom and Dad started to get out of their seats.

"I want to see her alone," I said. I wasn't able to see her in the hospital which made it so much worse. I kept imagining her with all these tubes in her nose and her arms and her head. I didn't know how they treated a stroke.

"You sure, Itzel? You don't want me to go with you?" Mom said, but she didn't get out of her seat.

"I'm sure. I want to talk to her. Just us."

Another nurse who was in the room turned from a table she was talking to and said, "Just so you know, sweetie, she's unresponsive," and I don't know what kind of look my family gave her, but the nurse quickly shut her mouth and went back to the other table.

"You go see your grandma," Dad said. "We'll be right here. She's in the Heart is Home room."

"Want me to hold your coat?" Mom said. I shook my head and made my way down the hallway.

The wallpaper in the hall had blue flowers with two white birds perched underneath the opening leaves. Bird after bird. Leaf after leaf. If I counted, there must have been a hundred before reaching Abuela. Most rooms I passed— Holiday Villa, Stairway to Heaven, Peace & Quiet—had their doors closed, except one. When I walked by Tiny Oasis all I saw was vase after vase of flowers. Red, yellow, blue, pink, but I didn't see anyone inside the room.

One nurse walked with another whose name tag announced *TRAINEE* and said,

"These people can't hear them," lowering her voice when she saw me pass nearby.

Heart is Home was painted on a wooden board the shape of a cloud. Abuela was under the white quilt we made together. Her feet towards the middle of the twin bed looked much too long. Her hair was behind her like sun rays, her lips dry and cracked, her hands at her side unlike when she was awake—they were always cooking or turning the pages in her prayer book, or caressing my hair as we watched *Wheel of Fortune* on Friday nights.

I heard Abuelos's cries echoing down the hall and I imagined Mom rubbing his back, her fingers over his spine repeating, *Papa, por favor,* asking him to calm down before we needed to get a bed for him too. Maybe that's what he wanted.

"I know you can hear me, Abuelita," I said, sitting on the bed next to her. Her veins were flat blue squiggly lines under her thin skin. "I know you can," I put my hand on hers. The slight warmth of them made me feel better.

Abuelita once told me that bodies may not always hear, but that the souls always did.

I gave her a kiss on the cheek and she exhaled. Her breath smelled like nothing. Not like the cafe con leche she had every morning, or the Aquafresh she swore by, or like the lipstick that looked and smelled like a taupe crayon. Her skin didn't smell of the rose perfume Mom and I got her for each of her birthdays from Woolworths either. I watched her eyes expecting them to flinch, for her hand to twitch, but there was no movement except for the slight rise of the blanket over her stomach.

She had always said she was going to go before Abuelo. That even though women tended to live longer, even though she didn't have diabetes like he did, she was going to go first.

"Abuela, it's Sunday." I got up from the bed, taking a bar of Hershey's chocolate from my coat pocket. I knew she heard me though she didn't move. I knew she smelled the chocolate there against the smell of nothingness in the room. I broke off two squares. Her square I broke into two.

I stood up and watched the door. No one was there and I knew no one would come because I was saying goodbye. Abuela's only grandkid was saying goodbye.

I took half a square of chocolate. One side smooth. I felt the ridges of the other side. Abuela was slightly propped up on two pillows. Her mouth was narrowly open. I put my hand on her chin and lowered it.

Her skin was smooth except where her mole was. I took the piece of chocolate and slid it between her teeth and cheek and made sure it stayed there, so she wouldn't choke. I fluffed the pillows under her head.

She had no reaction. She didn't smile. She didn't gag. I took my piece of the chocolate and put it on my tongue for it to melt. I held her hand and squeezed it when I saw her throat move. She was swallowing the melting chocolate. I wondered if she could taste it. If she knew it was Sunday. If she knew I was there.

I put my head on her stomach and felt her breathe. I took her hand and put it on my head, so she could feel my hair like she had so many times before. I felt her stomach rise once more, and put her hand back by her side. I kissed her forehead. I wrapped what was left of her piece, and the rest of the chocolate, and put it back in my coat pocket.

I didn't say goodbye.

When Mom and Dad took their turn to see her, I sat with Abuelito who fell asleep in the chair sitting up. I held his hand with my left and with the other I felt the chocolate soften as it melted there in my pocket.

Yours Faithfully

Right before Abuelo returned to Guatemala to live out the rest of his days in the house he and Abuela built, in the home they were both supposed to grow very old in, he took me to visit Abuela's grave one last time.

"I don't know how to pray, apparently, since Rosita isn't here anymore. I don't know if she can hear my prayers, so I wrote her a letter just in case."

It was raining and only the left wiper worked, and I wondered if this is how it was to be in a submarine.

"I need you to hold this," he said handing me an envelope. After he parked, he reached into the back of the car, pulling out an umbrella. It had bright miniature yellow ducks with green beaks. Abuela's initials etched into the wooden handle.

The path to her grave was a quiet one. Away from the traffic and many lights of the main streets it bordered.

"Don't worry about me," he said. "Just keep yourself and the letter dry."

I put the letter in the inside pocket of my jacket and held tightly to the umbrella as the wind was fighting to snatch it away. I followed Abuelo for a few seconds, winding around drowning tombstones and graves.

"Over here, Itzel." Abuelo knelt. His knees disappeared into the mud. I tried to cover him with the umbrella, but it didn't help. The rain was sideways now and pounced on him and his trembling hands as he wiped away some leaves stuck to Abuela's tombstone.

"Rosita, mi amor. I have something for you." I barely heard him though I knew he wasn't talking to me.

He bent his hands like shovels and started to dig to the right of the tombstone. Handfuls of mud and grass like Play-Doh were moved till a hole appeared.

"Ok, Itzel. The letter, please."

I took it from underneath my jacket and the rain hit it, but he grabbed it before it got too wet.

"Here you go, my love," Abuelo said, and kissed the letter, putting it in the hole. The blue ink began to bleed as it became drenched. He patted mud back on top and firmly pressed it down.

"Your Abuela. She loved letters. I never wrote them though, because I thought: Why do I need to? I live with her. Now, she is gone. I hope it's not too late. I hope she can read it in heaven." He began to cry.

"I'm sorry, Abuelo."

"Let's get you home, Itzel. Before you get sick."

And I helped him get up and we walked under the umbrella to the car. He took the handle and I saw him etching Grandma's initials.

On the way home. I watched the mud dry on his hands as he held on to the wheel.

Before and After

It wasn't long after Abuelo went back to Guate that Mom started to tell Tia Amelia Dad was different.

"Leonardo doesn't come home for dinner anymore. He says he works late, but he isn't getting paid more. When I press him, it's like talking to a wall."

I knew I shouldn't have been spying, so I was as quiet as could be and was careful not to step on that one wooden board that shrieked. There was a pause, and then she said, "He better not even think of going back to that. I'll call you later," and hung up.

I walked into the kitchen.

"Itzel. Please go tell your dad if he can't fix the garage door, I'll just call someone else to do it." Mom kept wiping her hands on the towel though they weren't wet. Dad never gambled before the heart attack, but once he came back, he'd started to do a lot of things he hadn't before.

"Dad, Mom said that the garage door isn't working again." I poked my head into the living room where he always sat on his green recliner and read the morning newspaper. It was the only thing that he ever did anymore that resembled what the fathers did on TV.

"I'll make sure it works!" he yelled out to Mom, whose grunts echoed in from the kitchen.

"You want to go over to Frijoles tonight with me?" He sipped his coffee and finally looked up. I hadn't noticed his mustache had grown in. I didn't remember it ever being that thick.

Everything is split now between Before the Heart Attack Dad and After the Heart Attack Dad. Before Dad played with me in the park and read me stories and told me that I should be a doctor because I was smart and I wouldn't have to struggle so much like he and Mom did. Before Dad laughed and told me jokes, ones he made up on the spot.

After Dad was different, like moving the lamp that had always been in the same corner to the other side of the room. It was the same lamp, but the light and shadows hit in a different way that made all that I was used to seem a little strange.

"Life. Life. Life," he repeated over and over once. "You have to live it. You have to make sure the choices you make are the same ones you'd make again when you look back ten, twenty years later."

I didn't know if he meant like where you bought a house, or the car you get, or where you work. But he'd say things like, "Don't regret anything. Don't die that way. Explore. Don't be afraid to try new things." I didn't know if he meant that for future me, or maybe he wished he would've married someone other than Mom. Maybe not have had me. Maybe be with someone else and childless, so that he could do all the things it sounded like he wanted to do and never did.

After Dad even looked different. He lost his beer belly; he was growing out the hair on his face. He liked to dress like he was going to church instead of Jewels. Mom at first liked it, but the more he did that the more he started to be out of the house. That's why even though there wasn't much to do at Frijoles' house, I didn't mind going. It made Mom feel better if I went with him, since she was allergic to Frijoles' cats and he and his wife, Doña Melinda, had more cats than cans of food.

"So, you want to go? We can ask Fred's mom if he can go with us, if you want." The steam from his coffee rising right between his eyes like the tip of his nose was smoking.

"Sure. I'll call Fred." I walked back into the kitchen. Mom was staring at Dad's work badge that was on the counter.

"You OK, Mom?" I grabbed the phone off the wall. The cord twisted and turned like a pretzel. The dial tone waiting for my command. I don't think Mom noticed me there. She just continued to shake her head like she did when she didn't know what to say.

Place Your Bets

The cats lived in different places in Frijoles' house. I was glad Fred came along this time, so I wouldn't be stuck watching TV with Frijoles' three kids who all picked their noses while watching *21 Jump Street*. They always had this gigantic Doritos bag between them. Eating some and throwing others at one another. And I'd sit there wishing I could sharpen a Dorito and throw one at their foreheads like a ninja star in a kung fu movie.

This was the first time Fred was at Frijoles', and when he saw one cat sleeping on the big fat television and another on top of the side table napping next to the fake flowers covered in dust, he looked surprised.

"There are more," I said and pointed to the dining room table. It was this huge wooden contraption with matching wooden chairs. Both the table and chair cushions covered in thick plastic. The chairs had been repainted instead of tossed from the wear and tear of years of three kids sitting, standing, jumping, farting, spilling, and knocking them over. The repaint hadn't been done by a professional.

Instead, Dad told me that Frijoles himself painted it construction-cone orange because that was what was on sale. He then had no choice to paint the table to match. On each of the six chairs was a cat. A couple had their tails hooked downward; others were only visible by the silhouette of their ears.

"Really?" Fred said. Somehow the house didn't smell like cats at all and instead smelled like Pine-Sol.

"Wait till you go in the basement," I whispered.

For now, we were in the living room with Frijoles' kids who were all on the couch watching, what else, *21 Jump Street*. They recorded the episodes on tapes and replayed them, each of them learning a part. They all wanted to be actors. All of them wanted to be Johnny Depp. That was never going to happen. After a while, I forgot their real names because they kept referring to themselves as Officer Hanson, and because Doña Melinda only called out to her sons as ¡Aye! (Somehow, they knew which ¡Aye! meant which kid.)

"Frijoles! You better not be smoking down there!" Doña Melinda screamed down the open basement door from the kitchen.

"Why do they call him Frijoles?" Fred leaned in and whispered. When did he start wearing cologne?

"His real name is Alfredo," I whispered back, wondering if he could smell my strawberry shampoo. "I remember him and his wife and my mom and dad used to hang out a lot when I was little. Mom told me everyone started calling him Frijoles after his wife knocked his teeth out with an iron when he lost another job from drinking."

Fred looked like he didn't know whether to laugh or take me seriously. I shrugged my shoulders. "That's what my mom told me."

Doña Melinda walked into the living room and we both jumped a little away from each other.

She had always been very nice to me. Always giving me pasteles and letting me drink coffee 'cause she said a girl my age back home picked the coffee and drank it three times a day by now. But today when I'd come to the door with Dad and Fred, she hadn't invited me into the kitchen to look at the magazines she always stole from her doctor's office so we could look at all the skinny gueras that didn't have an ounce of meat or brown on them. She said she couldn't do that any more with her three boys. They would look at the pictures for different reasons.

"Comadre, this is Fred. Itzel's best friend," Dad had said.

"Nice to meet you," Fred said and smiled. Doña Melinda didn't smile back. Instead, she looked right at him and then at me and then back at Fred, who then side-eyed me. Who knows where Dad was looking; with so many darting eyes, I got dizzy.

So Dad had gone straight to the basement to start his first game, and now Fred and I were squeezed in with all the kids on the red couch covered in plastic. Everything in the house was covered in plastic. The couch, the loveseat, the La-Z-Boy that Doña Melinda pronounced as *Lassie Boy*—plastic. Even the top of the TV, and the rug that was on top of the carpet in the middle of the room. The plastic on top of the rug made the white and black tiger look like it was glossy. Everywhere you went, you heard the crinkling of plastic.

After Fred got over the shock of all those cats, we started debating about who was better—Knight Rider or MacGyver—when Doña Melinda called me from the kitchen. The plastic on the couch screeched when I got up. Fred laughed.

When I went into the kitchen, I thought she was going to ask me what I wanted to drink or point to a model she found *as skinny as the magazine paper she was printed on,* but instead she glowered at me from behind the plastic-covered kitchen table. "You know," she said, "back in El Salvador I heard of a teenage boy and teenage girl who sat closely on the couch together and she ended up pregnant."

"Huh?" I already knew how babies were made because we'd had sex ed three years ago and Ms. Foster had showed us diagrams and charts. She had separated the boys and the girls, which I was glad because I heard the boys couldn't stop giggling—like little girls. I had also sat next to boys on couches before, so I was A-OK.

"Pregnant. That is when a baby is in your stomach." Doña Melinda leaned into me as though her words had somehow missed their mark.

"I know what pregnant means."

"Your mom is OK with you hanging out with *that* boy?" She crossed her arms. *21 Jump Street* sounds entering the kitchen.

Mom always told me to respect my elders, but the way Doña Melinda was saying *mom* like it was a roach, I didn't like.

I saw what she was going to serve for dinner. They were right there on the stove. "Doña Melinda, I see you made your famous tamales."

She turned as though she forgot she was upset and smiled. Her body loosened a bit.

"Hopefully they won't be as salty as last time."

Her eyes widened and her teeth bit her bottom lip. She probably looked like that when she grabbed the iron and gave Frijoles his nickname. Her mouth opened, but nothing came out. I walked back into the living room. Fred and I hadn't done anything wrong and here she was making me a mom at fourteen.

Fred was watching the cats more than the TV. One had curled up next to him. Probably hoping it wouldn't slip off of the plastic. It was as brown as Fred was. The kids were now yelling louder than ever. Doritos flying like yellow twisted birds.

"What did she want?" Fred said as I stood in front of him.

"Nothing. C'mon. Let's go downstairs to the canasta."

The canasta, aka Frijoles' basement, was covered not in plastic, but in wicker weave baskets that Doña Melinda bought at garage sales and the Salvation Army. There were mini ones that would be perfect for bird nests, round ones like cut out coconuts, huge ones that looked more like hammocks. They were stacked on top of one another in no real pattern from floor to ceiling all along the border of the basement.

The canasta was the only place the cats weren't allowed. Doña Melinda wanted to keep the baskets pristine, as she put it, though she pronounced it as *preston*. I think it was her only big English word and she used it a lot when she wanted to impress the folks that didn't know any English at all.

The poker table was made of six table trays pushed together covered in green felt. Dad said that Frijoles couldn't have a real table because the wicker baskets would pop up out of nowhere week-to-week. It was easier to move the makeshift poker trays around.

Neither Dad nor Frijoles nor the two other guys noticed us at the bottom of the stairs. They had music on real loud, Spanish versions of English 60s songs. Beer bottles were at everyone's feet. The guy with the button-up shirt covered in a pattern of dollar bills smoked so much I couldn't see his face in the dim lights.

Fred and I sat on the bottom step. His knee touched mine and I was about to move away because I felt myself turning red, but then I realized the light above the stairs was dim and even if he saw the red in my cheeks, he'd think it was blush, so I left my knee there. He didn't move his, either. Maybe he wasn't so worried about blushing. If Doña Melinda saw us, she'd probably tell me I was going to have twins.

We started to talk about how Mrs. Romero always looked angry except when Mr. Nowak, the gym teacher, came by to talk to her. (He wore these little navy blue shorts with a gym shirt that had the bouncing tiger logo of the school on the front. It was so faded all that was left were two stripes and one eye.)

"You! Boy! Come learn how to play a man's game!" We looked at the poker table.

Dad was staring at his cards and rubbing his chin. Frijoles was waving Fred over.

Fred turned to me and I shrugged my shoulders. "Time to be a man?"

He punched me in my arm.

"Come over and play. You have money, right?" Frijoles said as Fred got up and meandered over. I watched him squeeze in between Dad and the guy with orange sunglasses though the basement was windowless.

Dad gave Fred a five-dollar bill and said something, but it was hard to hear them over the cumbias. I was expecting Frijoles to say that girls weren't allowed down there, but that wouldn't fly with Dad, so no one said anything and I stayed, though I didn't get invited to play. I moved a little closer and sat on this huge woven basket with a flat bottom. Now, at least I was close enough to hear and see the table.

There were green, white, and red chips. A deck of cards that were Christmas-themed. I didn't think these grown men would be playing with Santa and Rudolph, but it was better than the cards that had naked girls on them, like the ones that Danny Trello got caught with at school.

Fred handed over the crinkled five-dollar bill to Frijoles, who was wearing this white visor. He gave Fred some white chips.

"You play poker before, young man?" the oldest man at the table asked Fred. "Richie," he said before Fred could even answer. "I'm Richie," he repeated and nodded to Fred.

"This here is Fred," Dad said and Fred nodded just like Ritchie had.

"I've never played before," Fred said while turning one chip in his hand.

"Your Dad never taught you?" the guy with the sunglasses asked. The smoke from his cigar was as thick as his accent.

There it was. Someone asked Fred about his dad. Some kids teased him in gym because he kept striking out. *Did your dad ever teach you how to hit the ball or is he just blind?*

Fred ignored Richie and instead snuck a look at me. I saw the brown that circled his pupils like the trees when their rings were exposed. I think he knew I wanted to play poker. Not that Dad wouldn't let me. He just didn't think of inviting me, that's all.

After two games, where Fred lost the five dollars Dad gave him and the next five dollars that Dad gave him, I decided I had hit my limit of counting the baskets and imagining all the different kittens and fruit that could go into each one.

"I want in," I said.

No one turned to look at me.

"I want in," I repeated and stood.

Frijoles looked at me and took a sip of his beer.

After we dropped Fred off, Dad said, "Don't tell your mother you played. She'll be extremely angry, and we both don't need that."

I nodded.

"That's all to say though, I'm so proud of you. Frijoles never saw that bluff coming. You got that from me."

I felt the $50 in my coat pocket. The bills smooth and soft between my fingers.

Royal Crown Cola & That Woman

The factory Dad worked at transformed the cafeteria into an Employee Appreciation Party Spectacular. That's what the hand-painted sign said that hung over the entrance doors. The cafeteria was covered with decorations that said *You're #1* taped on the walls, and crinkled streamers hanging from the still ceiling fans and the long tables under orange and white plastic tablecloths that were taped together in the middle.

After an hour of talking with some of the other kids, and all of us agreeing we were equally embarrassed by our parents and their dance moves, I took a break from playing Uno and went to get more soda. I stood at the table pouring out the warm RC when this woman came and stood next to me. Her dress was so low I saw the line where her boobs were pushed together, just like the line in the middle of Mom's forehead.

"My, you look like your daddy."

This woman was shaped like a toothpaste tube.

"You have Leo's eyes," she said, and pinched my cheek like the white-haired grandmas did on TV. I didn't know who she was or where she had come from. I glanced around and saw Dad and Mom still dancing. Mom's arms wrapped around Dad's neck, his behind her waist.

"I'm Nadine," the tall woman said, reaching out her hand.

I was brought up to be polite. I was also brought up not to speak to strangers. I didn't shake her hand.

"I work with your dad," she said.

I wasn't sure what I was supposed to say or what she wanted from me. Nadine smiled and patted me on the head like a dog and glanced over at my parents. The smile disappeared.

"See you around," she said, walking away to a group of people drinking beer from glistening bottles.

After another few rounds of Uno with this girl that looked like a red-headed Punky Brewster, I wanted some more of the pink wafers I had earlier, but there were none left on the table. This round woman, who had teeth so white that I saw the reflection of the party in them, told me there were more in the kitchen.

"Go help yourself. Just make sure to turn off the light when you're done. Chuck is cheap and gets mad if we leave them on." She pointed to the back of the room.

As people laughed and told jokes, as salsa blasted over the dwarf speakers plugged into the boom box that was all yellow and black like a bumble bee, as Mom talked to a group of women about how Dad had a heart attack on my thirteenth birthday last year, I went into the kitchen at the back of the cafeteria to get those delicious wafers.

I opened the door and began to feel around for a light switch and that's when I saw Dad and Nadine kissing under the moonlight that trickled in through the metal screens over the windows. They were in the corner of the room, their faces smashed into one another, Nadine so much taller than him, pale white in the moonlight.

I wasn't sure what to do. I shut my eyes tight to make it go away like erasing the wrong answer on a test, but I still saw them, still saw the wrong answer etched into the paper though the lead was brushed away. I stepped out of the room, letting the swinging door go back quietly in place as I walked back to the party.

The streamers were no longer bright and the music was noise and the laughs in the room were suffocating. I found Mom in the middle of a circle of women all gasping, so I knew that she was at the part where Dad was in surgery. I started to cry.

"Baby, what's wrong?" She stopped midway and I told her my stomach hurt and that I wanted to go home.

"Let me get your dad," Mom said, telling me to sit down. She hurried over to him. Nadine came up to me.

"I saw you chug that warm RC. Here's some that's actually cold." She tried to hand me a Styrofoam cup. I heard all those fake bracelets clink into one another like a hundred bells on a giant cat. I wanted to tell her what I saw. That I hated her, with her hair so blonde it was almost white, and her legs like trees. Instead, I shook my head and lowered my eyes to the floor until I heard her heels clack away.

When Dad asked me what was wrong all I did was cry some more and rub my stomach and say I wanted to go home. On the way to the car, Dad and Mom each held one of my hands like they hadn't in years.

In the Ring

The next morning, Mom had already left for her monthly Saturday shift. Dad was drinking coffee at the kitchen table while he watched Hulk Hogan wrestle.

"You feeling better, Itzel? Want some breakfast?" He didn't wait for me to respond. Instead, he got up and opened the fridge. "I'll make you some tea and toast."

"Thanks." I sat down and turned to the TV and saw someone had smashed another person with a steel metal chair just like the one I sat on the night before.

"Since your mom has to work today, I was thinking we'd pick up my check at the factory and go to the movies. I forgot to get it yesterday with all that was going on with the party. Later, we'll go pick up your mom." He pulled butter from the fridge.

"Sure."

He sat down across from me and drank his coffee. A couple times he pumped his fist when one wrestler threw another out of the ring. He looked at me and smiled. *With all that was going on with the party.* I tried to smile back the best I could.

When he finished his coffee and went upstairs, I threw my tea in the sink and the toast in the trash. On the way to the factory, I pretended to sleep in the car.

When we got to the factory, Dad gave me some quarters for the vending machine and went to the office to get his check. The vending machines were in the middle of the hallway, sandwiched between the door that led to all the machines where you needed to wear those special plastic glasses, and the door that led to the cafeteria. I was glad I didn't need to go back there.

"Well, hello there, pretty girl! You here with your dad?" Nadine smiled and I saw her perfectly squared teeth all smashed into her mouth. Her thin lips layered in dry lipstick, like pink cotton candy went there to die.

"No, my shift starts in ten minutes."

Nadine looked down at me with her blue eyes the color of those blocks that Mom throws in the toilet to make the water smell better. First, she giggled, but when she saw I didn't move, she stopped and put both hands on her non-existent hips.

"I know you are *fucking* my dad." I said *fucking* just like I'd heard in the Terminator movie. I had never cursed before and it sort of felt good, but I didn't show my pride or my excitement.

"What?" Nadine stretched out the word as though it had more than two syllables. Her lined eyebrows disappeared, and she tilted her head toward me like a deer catching a strange sound.

Out of the corner of my eye, I saw these two women with rubber gloves watching us, whispering to each other. I didn't know how long they had been there, nor if they heard what I said, but I no longer cared about getting in trouble. They could tell Dad that I had swore, but at least they'd have known what Nadine had done.

"You know what? You should have more respect in the way you talk to adults," Nadine said, lowering her head to my level. Her pores like pinpoints on an old map. Mom was so much prettier than her.

"Ah, I see you two are chatting!" Dad said all jolly, interrupting us. He didn't know what I had seen the night before, but now Nadine did.

"Leo, can I talk to you for a minute?" Nadine said.

"You know I don't talk *about work* on the weekends, Nadine. I just came to get my check."

Nadine nodded at him and then stared at me. I couldn't tell if what I said made her angry or scared of me. I didn't know if she wanted to say I'm sorry or smack me. I turned my back to her and glanced at Dad as we walked away. As we passed the two ladies, they stopped whispering and forced smiles. I heard the machines rumble as the door opened. Dad didn't look back once. I didn't know if Nadine was watching us walk away or had gone back to doing whatever she had been doing before. I didn't care. I felt like I had won...something. But that feeling was gone by the time we got to the car. Maybe I should've told Dad what I saw or even what I just said. It was Saturday, so I had two whole days till Nadine would see him again at work and tell on me. I had two days to figure out if I was going to tell Mom. Two days to figure out what to do.

"I thought you were getting some chips." He backed out of the parking spot.

"They didn't have what I wanted." It hit me that I wasn't just sad. I was mad. Real mad that Dad was part of this too. Dad must have wanted to kiss her.

Dad was turning up the volume on his oldies station, tapping his hands on the steering wheel as he pulled out of the parking lot. He looked left and right before we drove away from the factory. For a second, I thought maybe I had dreamt it all. Maybe it never happened and I just thought I did. Dad looked the same. His thick black hair curved at the end like waves. He smelled like the cologne Mom and I got him for Father's Day.

"Well, let's go get some lunch before we head to the movies. Too bad your mom had to work today. She doesn't like to work on Saturdays. You know, it's family day."

And that I did know. It was Saturday. Family day. And Mom wasn't here.

Screaming Silence

The car ride to McDonald's was the longest ride I ever had with Dad. Even longer than when he was called to come and get me at school in fifth grade because I punched Tina Martinez in the chest for calling me a nerd and tripping me. I got detention for a week because Tina fake cried, but I knew it didn't hurt because she stuffed her bra just like her mom.

"What do you want from McDonald's?" Dad asked while turning the corner and slowing down for a red light.

"What do you want with Nadine?" I wanted to say. Instead, I said, "Nuggets."

"Nuggets?" he looked confused.

I had never ordered nuggets in my life. I didn't understand the concept of eating tiny bits of chicken when you could have one whole piece.

I wanted to say, "Yeah, I never had nuggets before, but now I want nuggets. Do you want something now that you didn't want before?" But instead I said, "Yeah, nuggets."

"OK, then," he said, pulling into the parking lot.

What was I to say? Hey, Dad thanks for taking me to your factory party last night, but no thanks for making out with that ugly woman. Or: hey, you're the one who gave me the fake stomachache. I really just wanted to know why. Why would you cheat on Mom? Is this the first time? Do you even love Mom anymore?

I knew Dad would find out I knew on Monday when he saw Nadine. I didn't know if I was going to get in trouble, or if he was going to make me keep it a secret like the poker bet I won, or if he'd have me tell Mom because we both knew she didn't like them to argue in front of me and maybe it would give him time to make up an excuse or have him practice his sorry in English and in Spanish. None of those things had happy endings.

We were the next in line to order.

"Can I help you?" This teenage boy called us over as he adjusted the gray collar from his red polo. When we got to the counter, our eyes met and he smiled, and then stopped when he saw Dad was staring at him.

"I'll have a #1 combo and she'll have nuggets."

"I don't want nuggets. I changed my mind," I said, and I wanted to say, "You know, like how you changed your mind on staying faithful to your wife." Instead I said, "I'll have a #3."

We sat across from each other. The orange table smelled like bleach.

"Dad," I said, and he looked up from his Big Mac.

I was never one of those kids that looked just like their mom or just like their dad. I looked like both of them. Bits of Dad like his mouth and his lips, and bits of Mom like her green eyes and her thin eyebrows and her wide nose. I loved both my parents very much. They were both there for me and they both cared in their own way, and up until last night, I thought they felt the same way about each other.

"Dad," I repeated and I didn't know what to say or how to say it. "Thanks for lunch."

"You're welcome. How is it?"

"It's fine."

After we ate, we went to the Currency Exchange on Pulaski to cash his check. I noticed he grinned at the young woman behind the bulletproof glass a little longer than usual. A little longer than he would've smiled if it were a man, I think. He got his cash and put it in his wallet.

"Ready for the movies?"

I didn't want to go. I wanted to go home and call Fred and tell him what was happening, but he and his mom had gone to visit his grandma for the weekend. There was no way to reach him.

"Sure," I said. Maybe two hours in a movie theater not having to talk to him would be a good idea.

We saw *The Goonies*. It was about these kids that were going to lose their homes to some rich guy, so they go on an adventure while bad people dressed in black chased after them. And there was pirate treasure. It did help me forget a little. For a while, it was like everything was normal again. Dad bought us popcorn drenched in butter, and I caught us laughing at the same parts. But when it was over and the lights went up, I was back to not knowing what was going to happen to my family.

We always shared what we did or didn't like after seeing a movie. I didn't really feel like it, but I didn't want him to think something was wrong. I told him I liked that the weird looking guy ended up having a family in the end.

Then Dad went. "I liked that Mikey kept hope alive. He knew in his heart about the treasure. Be that way, Itzel. Always believe in yourself. Always have hope."

Mom was waiting for us outside the hospital. Her blue scrubs were fluttering in the strong wind. She waved when she saw us. When she got into the car, she put her purse in the backseat next to me and squeezed my face.

"How are you doing, baby? How was the movie?" and then she leaned over to Dad and they gave each other a peck on the lips like they always did.

"It was good. How was work?" And she started to tell us about one of the patients that kept spitting out his pills till they had to restrain him on a cot. She didn't like doing that, but it was necessary, she said.

While her and Dad got into a conversation about Tia Amelia, I tried to notice if their hands touched, or if they looked at one another while the car was at a red light. Any sign to see if Mom thought something was up.

"Itzel, how you feeling?" She turned to me even though the car was moving and she got motion sickness easily.

"It's better, Mama," I said, and I hadn't called her mama in a long time.

She turned back around to face the front, but I saw her smile. "Mama" she said.

Her arm was stretched out, her hand on the back of Dad's headrest. I saw her wedding ring in the sunlight. It was teensy enough to fit on one of my Barbie dolls, but she loved it just the same. Every Sunday she'd take off the ring and soak it in some warm water and Palmolive. After she'd take it out and wash it, she'd hold it up to the light. It sparkled when she put it back on.

Today, it looked dull.

A Long Night

Saturday afternoon dragged into Saturday night. Every time I looked at Dad, I was too angry and sad to say anything, the words a turtleneck inside my throat. We ate dinner while watching a movie about a family that adopts all these kids. Dad was on his recliner and I was next to Mom on the couch. They seemed fine.

I couldn't stop thinking of why Dad would do that to Mom. I didn't get it. They usually seemed happy, but something did change after the heart attack. Maybe I didn't see it then, whatever *it* was. I wished Abuela was still here.

The screen became a blur and I wondered if maybe Mom and I weren't enough family for him. I remembered hearing them talk a few years ago, when they thought I was asleep. *Maybe the third pregnancy will be successful*, Dad said. I didn't understand what he meant back then, but now I was older. I was an only child. Why did Dad say third?

The movie finally ended and we all went to bed. I waited until I heard them both snoring and got out of my bed. The snores got louder as I got closer to their room.

Just inside their bedroom was the closet. Behind their shirts and pants and dresses, hidden in the corner, was the black hard suitcase with the silver clasps like the ones used in bank robberies in the movies. I knew Mom kept the important stuff in there. I knew everything that I ever needed to know about my parents was in that suitcase.

I peeked my head into the room and saw Mom facing the window, her back to me, and Dad on his back with his mouth wide open. I had never snuck into their room before and it wasn't as exciting as I thought. I was nervous to get caught and I didn't even really know what I was searching for. I parted the hanging clothes but froze when I heard one of them cough. Finally when the snoring started again, I reached out into the dark shadows and felt around until the handle was between my fingers. I slid it out and lifted it. It was heavier than I thought, but I held it close to my chest and tip-toed out of the room.

Back in my room, I turned on my lamp and sat right under it on the rug. There in the briefcase were Mom and Dad's lives on sheets of papers. Papers that said she and Dad were citizens. My birth certificate that said I was theirs. A sheet with a stamp on it that said they owned the house we lived in. There were photographs of back home that showed my great-grandma in front of the most miniature house I had ever seen, like it belonged to the munchkins in *The Wizard of Oz*. A baby blanket I didn't remember lined the bottom. The **A B C** in bold colorful letters surrounded by old-looking gray stitched squares. There was nothing in that suitcase that felt like it was the answer.

I was worried I was cutting it too close but I checked the flap on the side and felt a plastic sleeve. I pulled it out to find a picture. A baby in a white dress and an oversized white matching bonnet in a casket. There was no one around the casket.

I knelt and brought the picture closer to the lamp. I saw the reddish brown of the wood. The flash off of the gloss. It looked like a baby doll whose eyes open when you pick it up. Its lips floating above its face. I couldn't tell if it was a boy or a girl. Or why it was dead. Or why Mom had a picture of it hidden in her special suitcase.

1974 was scrawled on the back. Two years before I was born. They had never told me about this. What else haven't they told me?

I put the picture back and snapped the suitcase shut. My mind had been racing since I saw Dad with Nadine and now so many more thoughts were pushing into one another making my head hurt. I was in and out of the closet again with no problem. Their snores swirling around like my thoughts until I finally fell asleep.

Holy Advice

The next day, Mom and I picked up Tia Amelia and we went to church. Dad had been too tired to go to church with us for the last few weeks. Mom and Tia Amelia liked to sit in the middle pew right off to the side. They said it was close and far enough away from the altar.

During the first reading, I took a real look at the church. I'd had my baptism, communion, and confirmation here. Mom and Dad got married here. Dad said it was an intimate wedding because they couldn't afford more, but Mom said *why do you need a lot of people when it's about two*. She said the day they got married it stormed all day. The church lights were too soft for them to really see each other.

The sun was bright this time. The glass-stained windows seemed to cast odd-shaped rainbows above the pews. There were a couple of kids chatting in the row in front of me. Their faces turned to one another. Their lips moved slightly. Whispers of whispers. I couldn't hear what they were saying.

Father Joe was giving his sermon and when he said that forgiveness was a gift that should be given, I almost laughed and cried at the same time. What was Dad doing right now while we were here? Was he on the phone with Nadine? Does she know when to call? Was she telling him right now what I saw and said?

After communion came announcements. Father Joe reminded everyone of the pancake breakfast and that he'd be in the front pew after mass in case anyone wanted to talk.

"You don't have to confess," Father Joe said. "You can just talk. Sometimes we all need someone to talk to."

"I got us some pancake breakfast tickets," Tia Amelia said.

"Can I meet you guys down there? I need to go to the bathroom," I said.

Tia Amelia gave me my ticket and they headed towards the back of the church. When they went left, I went right towards the bathroom. As soon as they were out of my view, I turned back and hurried towards the front pew.

Each empty pew looked ancient. Wood all worn. Father Joe's back to me as he faced forward. Strands of white like dental floss on the back of his head.

He made the sign of the cross over a bible someone was holding. Some woman around Mom's age. She returned the sign and put the bible close to her chest and walked past me. Smiling at me when our eyes met.

"Hello Father Joe." I stood next to the pew. He glanced up from his bible and smiled at me. The thin wrinkles around his eyes curved.

"Itzel. Welcome." He closed his bible and put it on his lap. "What can I help you with?"

I didn't know what I wanted to tell him or how much or if I should. He knew both my parents. Went to all our family functions though he never stayed much longer after the blessing of the food. Just long enough to eat, but never long enough to hear the *cumbias* turned up so loud the big speakers shook, and everyone yelling at each other to be heard. Once Father Joe left, that's when the tray of shot glasses came out and all the adults started drinking to the memory of someone who passed, or to someone's birthday, or simply because there was oxygen in the room.

"I may have seen something I shouldn't."

"I see."

I sat down and didn't want to look at him. I didn't want to see pity in his eyes once I told him what had happened. I stared at the wooden cross that hung above the altar.

I started rubbing my face as if trying to take off the image of Dad there, but when I opened my eyes again, all I saw was Jesus, and then I couldn't understand why God wanted my family to break up so bad. First Dad had the heart attack and Mom said God saved him, but then who wanted him to almost die in the first place? Now Dad was healthy and he was with someone else. I didn't get it.

Father Joe stared straight ahead too. I could see him out of the corner of my eye.

"My father isn't the same as before."

"Leonardo is different in some ways, yes."

"He may not want to be with my mom, anymore," My throat went dry.

"What makes you think that?" Father Joe said in a tone that made me want to tell him why.

"I saw him kissing someone else at his company's party."

"I see."

"I don't know if I should tell my mom. I don't know how this will change things."

Silence sat with us for a few seconds.

"Itzel. Your father and your mother love you both very much. It's a lot to ask of yourself to keep this secret, but it's also a lot to expect you to tell and then watch the consequences unfold. Though they wouldn't be because of what you said."

The glass-stained windows were now colorless.

"I don't know what to do."

"Maybe ask him to explain. I'm not saying what he did was right, but if anyone should tell your mother, it should be him. Give him a chance to explain to her."

I finally looked at Father Joe. He looked at me.

"Itzel, I'm sorry the world isn't like it should be."

"Father," I heard behind us and there was an old woman there with a rosary in her hand.

"Thanks for listening," I said and walked past the woman.

She didn't seem to see me there.

Quiet Sunday Afternoon

Dad had just gotten out of the shower when we got home. His hair was dripping on his shirt. Mom gave him a kiss.

"Amelia is coming over for lunch later, but I just realized we don't have an onion for the rice. Do you mind going to pick one up?"

"Sure thing. Want to come with, Itzel?"

"Sure thing," I said, just as he had.

In the store, he told me to pick the onion while he went and picked a pie for dessert. He said he was in the mood for pie. He said it just like that, *I am in the mood for pie,* and maybe it's because Butera was playing some sad-sounding song without the words or because he left me alone to get the one thing Mom asked him for, but I started crying right there holding a sweet onion in my hand.

I didn't even try to hide it. I didn't even use my one free hand to wipe the tears away. I just let the tears fall and fall, so much so that I watched the bottom of my pants turn a darker blue. The white tile glowed there under my bubbly tears. I didn't know if I could go the whole day without telling Mom. Without telling Dad. I didn't know how to tell him I knew.

"You OK, honey?" This old lady with thick red glasses and a matching chain stood there. Her hands on a cart filled with Twinkies. Not boxes of Twinkies, but individual Twinkies. About fifty of them in the cart all lined up next to each other like they were in some kind of Twinkie military.

"It's the onion," I mumbled. I knew she knew I was lying.

"Ah. Yes. Those darn onions. They tend to sneak up like that. But remember, crying cleanses the soul." She squeezed my arm and then reached into her purse and pulled out a handkerchief that was ivory with yellow daisies sewn into each corner.

"It's clean. Go on. Take it."

I took it and wiped my eyes. I tried to give it back, but she shook her head.

"Keep it, honey." She walked away, grabbing an avocado as she passed.

Dad came back with an apple pie.

"Is that the one your mom wanted?"

He didn't ask about my red eyes, or the strange handkerchief I was holding.

Hop On

Fred was waiting for me in front of his house like always so we could walk to school together. His book bag over one shoulder, his green hat pulled down, faded on the edge of the bill. Now that we were in high school, our moms stopped freaking out about us walking to school on our own. They kept thinking we'd get kidnapped, and on the first day of school, we'd even caught them riding along real slow in the Buick. Anyone from far away would've thought they were a couple of ladies trying to kidnap us.

"So, do you want to go to Duke's after school?" Fred said. We stopped by the burger joint almost every week, dousing our fries in ketchup that we shared, along with a soda packed with ice. The ringing of the bell above the door sounded like Morse code as kids came and left. I just stopped in my tracks.

"My dad's having an affair," I said, and it was the first time I had said it out loud. It left a metal taste on my tongue.

"What?" He stopped.

"On Friday, I saw him kissing this woman he works with at the factory party. He doesn't know what I saw. My mom doesn't know either."

"Fuck." He swore every chance he got when our moms weren't around, but this time he didn't do it just to do it. He didn't know what to say, and I didn't know what to do but cry.

The first time I cried in front of Fred was when we were ten years old. We were in his backyard so we could play, and I saw a bruise the size of Asia on his arm. I poked at it, thinking that it must have been makeup like I had seen in the monster movies.

We were in our makeshift tent, built by an old comforter that was brown and white, a jaguar on it like it wanted to pounce, draped over two large branches on the only tree in his backyard. The bruise seemed to throb there in the little light that entered as we lay on our backs in the grass, our arms behind our heads, with a bowl of gummy worms between us.

"How'd you get that?"

"My dad," he whispered, then told me what happened.

I didn't want to see it, but I did. Mr. Costa choking Fred's mom, before Fred yelled at him to stop, and then Mr. Costa turning on Fred.

I started to cry for Fred, right there on the grass under the thick comforter, with the sun only peeking through the sides like jelly out of bread.

"Don't cry."

"I don't want you to be hurt."

Fred sighed and started crying though he wouldn't let me see. He just turned his head away.

And now instead of being fourteen, I felt like we were little and back under that makeshift tent all over again. Only this time it had to do with me.

"My dad's having an affair. I saw him," I repeated.

Fred became waves through my eyes and he grabbed my hand and led me in between two buildings. These little chihuahuas barked at us from behind a gate, and I wished I could disappear.

"OK," he said. That's all he said. "OK," Fred repeated and I knew he was thinking how he could fix this. I was his best friend, and that was the job of a best friend.

"C'mon, we're skipping school," he said. He pulled me along with him back towards his house. His mom would've already left for work.

I wanted to ask what about school, but no one there noticed too much. We had a field trip anyway, and our teachers would've just thought our parents wouldn't let us go.

Everything looked glossed over. The trees and the fences, even the graffiti of big blue bubble letters that spelled *FESTER* seemed to float there on the cement wall.

He slid his key into his front door and threw his book bag down on the kitchen floor. "You don't need to cry anymore, Itzel."

He poured us some orange juice. The light through the kitchen window fell across his face in one brush stroke and the darkness of his skin was like Kit-Kats.

I wiped my eyes.

"Hungry?" he said, already yanking the bread from its steel box and tossing two pieces into the toaster.

"What am I supposed to do? Tell my mom about my dad and Nadine?"

"Is that her name? Nadine? What kind of name is Nadine?" He popped the bread out of the toaster after only a few seconds and knifed slabs of butter onto it so fast the chunks didn't even have time to melt, and he gave me a slice.

"My mom is prettier than her." I took a bite of the bread.

"Looks don't matter. That's what my mom said anyway, when my dad left. Looks don't matter. It's that the woman is different, like a new toy or a new comic book or something. It's all exciting because it's never been opened."

I chuckled. He chuckled too.

"I'm sorry about your dad, but you'll be OK."

I knew he was right. He had gone through it and he was OK, and eventually I'd be too.

"C'mon, let's go into the living room. There's something I want you to check out. And it'll give us some time to figure out what to do next."

I sat down where I always did on the large brown sofa, right in the corner where I could sink in. He seemed a little nervous, but grabbed a piece of paper off the piano that his mom had bought him from a secondhand store.

"OK." He plopped on the couch next to me. "I wrote a song."

"Are you going to sing me a song?"

"No, it's a sonata. I'm going to be a composer."

"I didn't know that."

"You're the only one who does now. So I don't have all the instruments, of course, but I'll try to sound out the piece for you." He straightened his back and took a deep breath. He slid his finger across notes that dipped and curved and rose. Some short and some long, over lines and lines on the sheet. And I ended up closing my eyes so I could really hear it. Hear the orchestra there, like a hundred times bigger than the band at school with the violins and horns and drums.

At that moment, I wanted to kiss him like I had seen on TV. I had never kissed anyone before. I had never wanted to kiss anyone before. And I had never seen Fred like a boy that I'd actually want to kiss, and here we were in his living room on the couch I'd sat on so many times before when both of our families were happy, sitting here after telling him about my dad and Nadine, with dried tears on my face, and butter on my lips, and the mowing of a lawn down the block. I wanted Fred to look at me and see me as a girl he'd want to kiss.

He was still sounding out, humming, using his free hand to conduct the middle of the empty living room where the sun took a nap on the plush green rug. I was safe there and for a second, I made myself not think about my dad or my mom, or how our family was going to change, and I didn't think about how my Tia Amelia sometimes cried for her family, or how Fred and I would graduate high school in three years and who knows where we'd go after that. It was just him and his music that he wanted to share with me.

He finished the piece and we looked at each other and then I panicked. What if he was going to kiss me? He had kissed Betty Martinez before summer break last year out behind the school, when she told him she wanted to and he said OK because he was curious.

"Her tongue was slapping me in the face," he had told me, and I was just in shock that she used her tongue.

What if he kissed me and my tongue didn't move, or it moved too much, or his tongue and mine fought because we couldn't figure out where to go like when I'm walking down the halls in school and I turn the corner and there is someone else turning the corner too going the opposite way and then we do this side-to-side thing because no one knows which way to go to get out of the way of the other, so instead we are both in the way. What if it was like that?

Fred finished and put the paper on his lap. I hadn't noticed how it was all in pencil. I saw the parts where he erased the notes and put them in other places, and where he colored in the notes so much they looked like chocolate chips had fallen on the page.

"Fred," I said. "I've never kissed anyone before," is what I thought I said, but I guess I didn't because he said, "Thanks, I'm glad you liked it."

Fred got up and put the paper back on the piano. "Guess what? I found out my dad is in town. He's at Mancho's."

Mancho was this guy that used to work with his dad. That wasn't his real name, but I don't think anyone knew what his real name was. I remember being over for a family party and Mancho got so drunk off a 24-pack of Corona he threw up in the plastic kiddie pool that Fred and I used to cool off our feet.

Fred said: "I want to ask him why he hurt my mom and me. Why did he leave instead of changing? Want to come with me? Then if you want, we'll go to the factory and you can ask your dad the same thing."

He'd gotten me to stop crying and told me everything was going to be OK and shared his sonata with me. And all he wanted was for me to go to him, so he could ask his father why. Why he had left without saying goodbye. How he had left so easily. And I wanted to know why, too.

We hopped on the Grand bus. We flashed our school passes, covering our names as though the bus driver really was going to stop the bus and get on that huge green phone and report two kids that weren't in school. But we covered our names anyway, and he just looked at them and then at us and shut the doors and pulled away from the curb.

We bounced all the way to the back. There was this old man we passed who had a cart with empty paper bags stacked on the bottom. When he saw us he clenched the handle.

Since the whole back of the bus was empty, Fred took the middle seat in the last row. I sat down a seat over since his legs had sprouted and I thought he could use more room. He then slid a seat over and was right next to me.

"So, what's up with Norman?"

"Norman? From Chemistry?"

"Yeah. Did you kiss him yet?" Fred laughed.

"What? No. Why would I?"

Norman was this kid that never washed his glasses and always made sure his hand was raised even before the teacher asked a question.

"He likes you," Fred said and I saw a flash of his braces. All of a sudden, I really loved braces.

"No, he doesn't, and it doesn't matter." I rolled my eyes, wishing he'd change the subject.

"Why, you like someone else?" Fred said, and he leaned forward, so I couldn't avoid his face. There it was. That face in front of my face, inches apart and for a second, I wondered if this was how Dad and Nadine started. Out as friends and then one day they were sitting in the car when he drove her home and one face was in front of the other.

"What's wrong? I was just teasing," Fred said. "You thinking about your dad?" He put his hand on top of mine and said, "I'm sorry." His lips parted as though he wanted to say something else, but they closed again. We rode the rest of the way in silence. Each staring out our own windows.

Ask Why

Mancho lived off the tracks on Grand near Harlem, right above this pet clinic with a rabbit and a dog and a cat silhouetted on the sign.

"What if he's not here?" I glanced up at the windows with dirty white curtains.

"He *has* to be here," Fred said.

I didn't know who had told him he was there, and I was pretty sure it wasn't his mom, or we wouldn't have been there to begin with.

Fred pushed the doorbell, which had a piece of tape above it that looked like the ones they used on bandages. The ink smeared stain of a last name. We waited.

Fred glanced up and was about to press it again when, through the locked glass door, we saw loafers descending the stairs. We both looked at each other and took a deep breath at the same time. By the time we looked back, Mancho was standing there unlocking the door from the inside.

"I want to see my dad," Fred said, before the door was completely opened.

"Nice to see you too, Freddy," Mancho said, and I knew this was going to be bad because the only person that ever called Fred 'Freddy' was his dad.

"I want to see my dad. I know he's here," Fred stood taller and stared right into Mancho's eyes.

"Oh, you know that, huh?" Mancho glared over at me like he recognized me but didn't want to bother wasting time trying to remember from where. "He's not here, Freddy. He hasn't been here since he left." And it sounded like he wanted to add you guys or his family or you and your mom, but he stopped at left.

"I know he's here," Fred said, but even I knew that he wasn't. Whoever'd said his dad was back in town was lying, or maybe Fred heard what he wanted to hear.

"You need to go home, Freddy. Take care of you and your mom." Mancho shut the door and locked it before Fred found anything else to say.

We ended up across the street at the bus stop going back the way we came. I caught Fred peering up at the curtains to see if they moved, to see if he'd catch his father peeking behind them, but I think he knew at that point that he wasn't there.

We saw the bus coming and I took out my pass, but he grabbed it away from me.

"Hey," I said.

"We're going to see your dad." He started to walk across the street, back to the other bus stop.

I chased after him.

"I don't want to see my dad." My whole body turned into itself. Maybe they just kissed that one time. Maybe Dad had confessed to Mom and she'd forgiven him because she goes to church and isn't that what Father Joe preaches about every Sunday? And maybe they didn't tell me because it's grown stuff and I was going to ruin everything by making Dad confess to me and I wasn't really sure what forgiveness was, so how was I supposed to do that?

"You need to find out why," Fred said and looked down the empty street for the bus.

"No, I don't," I said.

"Yes, you do, Itzel."

"No. I. Don't. Fred."

"Well, you are."

"Why?"

"Because you can," he yelled. He had never yelled at me angry before.

"You can see your dad. You can ask him why. Don't you understand?" And then he sat on the bench and cried. It was like that moment in the tent when neither of us knew what to say, but unlike that moment he didn't turn away from me.

"I'm scared." I sat down next to him. He took his green hat and kneaded the bill into a curve with his hands. He always wore that hat. It used to be his dad's. What if my dad decided he wanted to leave, too? What was he going to leave behind for me?

"We don't have to go," Fred said, wiping his eyes. The bus was coming.

"No, let's go see him," I said and wrapped my arms around him. He hugged me back.

We boarded the bus.

The security guard didn't even look at me like we weren't supposed to be there midday on a Monday. Dad had been working there since '67, so he knew I was Leo's daughter. He waved us in and went back to reading what looked like a *TV Guide*.

It was Dad's lunch hour. The time hadn't changed for all the years he worked there. When Mom was laid off, he'd call her every day at noon, so she could tell him what rerun she watched that morning while making brunch.

"Ok," I said out loud, but not really to Fred. I was going to lead us right to the cafeteria where Dad would be eating the lunch Mom made him that she put in the new Tupperware with the green lid.

We walked down the long corridor and the tile squeaked under our gym shoes. I saw bits of cardboard scraps on the floor.

Fred didn't say anything. He walked next to me, looking around at the posters on the walls and doors. Most were about safety, with the big warning signs to be diligent when you worked. One sign had this chainsaw-looking machine, and an arm coming off with a lightning bolt between it and the stick person. **ZAP!** drawn like on the old Batman show I watched on Tuesday nights.

What if Dad was eating lunch and Nadine was next to him? What if she was not only next to him, but she was eating from the Tupperware with the green lid too? I imagined one of those signs that showed her reaching into the Tupperware and a lightning **ZAP!** between my hand and her face.

I smelled a mixture of pepper and pizza and grease. I saw some workers eating at the round tables, and since I knew most of them, they just turned and waved at me. I waved back, searching around for Dad.

"Leo went home for lunch," someone yelled.

I couldn't remember the last time Dad had gone home for lunch. Fred and I nodded. We still didn't say anything to each other when we left the factory and made our way back, but we both knew to run the two blocks when we got off the bus.

But by the time we got to my house, he was gone.

Kiss & Tell

We left our book bags on the floor and sat on my couch this time and turned on the TV. Some soap opera came on where this guy and this girl each had the same humongous hair. They peered at each other and then started kissing. I peeked over at Fred to see if he was looking at me, but all he did was look at the TV. He was all cool about it, with his hands on his knees, leaning back into my couch that wasn't as comfortable as his.

Mom and Dad told me I couldn't date till I was sixteen. They told me that boys could wait and study came first, and though they knew I was mature for a fourteen-year-old, taking advanced classes and all, I had *just* turned fourteen. Boys could wait.

But they also told me they loved each other. And to respect other people. And there was Dad kissing another woman.

I turned and stared at Fred. I heard the girl on TV giggle and I wondered if Fred liked the way she giggled and if I giggled cute like that.

"I want to kiss you," I said, as though I was telling him I wanted some chips.

"What?"

"You heard me. Kiss me. You kissed Betty Martinez and you weren't even friends with her."

"Itzel," he said, and that's all he said. He didn't move or look away. He just said my name one time, and I wasn't sure if I was to fight or flight like they talked about in biology class.

"Fine, forget it," I wanted to cry again, but I didn't. "Fine," I repeated and turned my body to the TV.

"I kissed Krystal," he blurted.

"Krystal? Krystal Rabbani?" I wanted to throw up for real.

"Yeah." He dropped his head.

Of all people, why did he kiss Krystal Rabbani?

Krystal Rabbani moved into the neighborhood when we were in third grade. She was this thin, blue eyed, blonde girl that everyone thought was *the prettiest little girl anyone had ever seen.* When my mom heard that, she rolled her eyes and told me I should be grateful that I had skin that wouldn't burn in the sun.

In eighth grade, she started to hang out more with the older girls, and the boys paid more attention to her in class, probably because she got these little boobs that looked like she put two Dunkin' Donuts Munchkins under her shirt. I didn't have any boobs at all in eighth grade when all the girls started to, and even Tommy Diaz was bigger than me, but that's because he had a metabolism problem or juvenile diabetes or something.

I was way smarter than Krystal, but she was prettier, I guess. Her hair was blonde and long and straight, and mine was huge and frizzy and all over the place. I knew she started liking Fred when on the first day of eighth grade she pretended to drop her pencil on the floor so he could pick it up for her. He had thought she was conceited and never paid attention to her before, but he wasn't rude, so when he picked it up and gave it to her, she touched his face all slow about it and said, "Thank you, Freddy."

"Freddy? What the fuck?" I'd mumbled.

"I dunno," he said, but I saw him watch her walk away.

"Why didn't you tell me?"

"Because you hate her," Fred said, and he had a point.

"When?" I looked at the clock on the wall as though it was going to transform into a time machine and I could go back and change what happened.

"After school last year. That one day you were sick." He stared past me, towards the empty vase by the window.

I remembered that day, only because I never got sick, and that time I had gotten the stomach flu, which Fred gave to me, actually.

"So, you kissed and..." I glared at him. I wasn't sure why I was so mad, and I wasn't sure why he wasn't mad that I was mad, but I did what Mom did when she fought with Dad. I kept the argument going.

"And nothing. That was it."

Then I got mad for real. I wanted to scream. I wasn't sure whom I was mad at though. Krystal *was the prettiest girl in the whole neighborhood* and Fred was Fred. And then there was me.

"So you don't want to kiss me, but you'll kiss Krystal Rabbani?" I took a deep breath and got off the couch and stood.

"I didn't say I didn't want to kiss you." And for the first time since the whole kiss question came up, he looked at me.

And then I went from wanting to throw the pillow at him for kissing Krystal Rabbani, to wanting to throw myself at him. Fred was going to kiss me. What did that mean? Like, it was cool when I thought he had only kissed one girl. Betty Martinez was gross, but now he had kissed two. Two! What if he liked the way they kissed better?

Then what if things changed? Fred and I had been friends for so long.

But then I really wanted to kiss him.

He got up off the couch and stood in front of me where I was by the TV.

"I'm nervous," I said.

"Me too."

"You don't have to kiss me. It's stupid."

"I've been wanting to. I just didn't know if you did." He had his hands in his pockets, and I wondered how he stood with the other two girls.

We moved closer together. I went on my tiptoes and put my hands behind his neck. His skin was so soft and the bottom of his fade brushed my fingertips and I swallowed so hard I thought it was going to echo through the house.

Out of the corner of my eye, I saw the flashing of the TV, and the sun streaming into the windows, and the couch where we had just sat moments before when I thought this was never going to happen. And now he had his hands around my waist and they felt perfect there.

His eyes glittered like pencil shavings. I tilted my head up, he brought his down, and his lips touched mine. Oh, man. His lips were touching my lips.

They were gentle and sweet and I couldn't remember if I had put on any Chapstick, and were mine as gentle and sweet to him? His mouth was wet and his tongue slid into mine and it wasn't like anything I had ever felt. It wasn't like running into someone in the hallway.

I don't know how long we had been kissing, but when we stopped, we let go and stepped back, stared at one another, and laughed.

"That was nice," he said, and I was a little surprised he said it first.

I said, "Yeah, it was," then I put my hand on my waist and said, "Better than Betty Martinez? Better than Krystal Rabbani?" and though I was laughing, I really just wanted to hear him say it.

"Yeah, much better than both. I'd like to do that again," he said, and then right when I was about to say yeah, he looked out the window and said, "But maybe later, cause your mom and dad are home."

I saw the car getting closer and rushed to turn off the TV. My gym shoe caught on the rug and I almost fell to the floor. Fred scrambled to get our book bags, and he yanked my hand as we ran out of the living room. We just made it out, shutting the kitchen door. The wind hit us as we crouched down and listened at the back door. I thought I heard the keys in the front door and footsteps in the house.

Maybe they had just come home early from work to spend time together. Maybe Mom felt sick at work and she called Dad to bring her home. Maybe everything was all right.

But they just started yelling.

"Leo, what's going on with you?"

I was too afraid to stand and peek through the window.

"What are you talking about?" Dad said, and then said something in a lower voice I couldn't make out.

"Let's get out of here, Itzel," Fred whispered, but I didn't move.

"You've changed! Talk to me!" Mom shouted.

"I don't know what you're talking about!" Dad's voice sounded closer to the door.

"What is happening with you, Leo?"

Those were the last words Fred and I heard. Then there was nothing but the branches creaking in the trees.

The back door began to rattle, and Fred and I sprung off the steps and darted around the side of the house. I peeked over and saw Dad standing on the step we'd just been sitting on, and I wondered if he could feel our heat there in the cold sun. He took out a cigarette and lit it, took a deep drag, and glared back at the house.

It seemed like he wanted to go back in. The top of his body turned toward the door, but his feet were facing forward. Dad took a step away from the house and with his head down, he wandered into the yard, the smoke fading above him. He turned around the other side of the house to go to the front. Just before I lost sight of him, I thought he looked like a bear. His coat thick and bulky and brown.

I heard the car start but not drive off, and I didn't know if he was waiting for Mom to come out, or if I should go tell her that he was still there, or if maybe I should go to him myself.

The engine growled out front. Fred and I leaned against the side of the house. I stared at his hat. The edges around the bill were coming undone. "I think I know how you feel now," I said.

"I'm sorry," he said. "I don't want you to get hurt."

"I don't want you to, either."

Fred grabbed both of my hands in his. Our palms were the only thing that felt warm. We heard the engine rev higher as my dad backed out of the driveway.

Together, we peered around the corner and watched the car go out of sight.

Out In the Open

Later at dinner Mom asked me how school was, and told me Dad was working late. She said she was tired and headed to bed early, and I went to bed soon after that but didn't sleep. Sometime later when I was finally dozing off, I heard the stairs creak and then the front door shut. I peeked out my bedroom window and saw Mom there in the driveway, the streetlamp hitting her pajamas and a coat that was Dad's. The neighbor's dog barked, and the cats with the glowing eyes that always sat across the street on my neighbor's couch both watched Mom get into the car as though they were wondering where she was going too.

I went downstairs and saw Tia Amelia on the couch. The TV was on, but her eyes were closed. She had her hands inside the front pocket of her hooded sweatshirt. Her feet in gym shoes that still had some snow on them.

"Tia, where did my mom go?"

She opened her eyes, not startled nor mad. She simply said, "You should be sleeping, Itzel."

I knew Tia Amelia was holding back and she didn't like to lie. She could withhold the truth, but not straight out lie.

"Tia, if I guess, will you tell me if I'm right?"

She nodded. Tia Amelia and I were close, even closer since her family died. She came over more often, and she thought I couldn't hear her cry to Mom and Dad when I was supposed to be sleeping, but the walls in our house were thinner than skim milk.

I sat on the couch with her and crossed my legs. The living room tended to be cold since one of the windows was cracked. The television was on *Family Feud*, Richard Dawson's hair so white. I heard the *ding* as someone smacked the button to blurt an answer.

I knew my dad was in trouble because Mom went outside in her pajamas. Mom never went anywhere in her pajamas. She prided herself on always looking presentable because you never knew who you were going to run into.

"Did my mom go get me a birthday present?" I knew the answer to this one, but I needed to see if this question-and-answer thing was going to work.

Tia Amelia shook her head, her short hair curled up slightly where it touched her neck.

"Is my dad in jail?" I didn't know what my dad could've done to go to jail, but for a moment I was scared that he was. Maybe one of his poker games had gone bad because I wasn't there. He said I brought him luck, that's why he usually took me. Maybe he lost all his money and then ran out of gas and he had to walk home and then some mean guys in leather vests beat him up and he had to fight back and he killed one of them by poking them in the eye with his keys.

"That'd be better," Tia Amelia said.

I knew Dad wasn't hurt in the hospital somewhere with a missing leg, or water in his lungs, or all bloody hit by a car, because we'd all be driving to the hospital like when he had the heart attack.

And then I knew where he was. I knew where Mom had gone and why. And why it would've been safer for Dad to be behind bars where Mom couldn't get to him.

"Is he with that tall blonde woman from the factory?"

Tia Amelia let out a long sigh. "Yes, your father is with that woman."

Applause. I looked at the TV. This family, all in matching red shirts, jumped and hugged each other.

I imagined Dad and Mom there and Tia Amelia and me, being together and happy and jumping, clapping. All of us happy.

"So my mom knows?" I said, still staring at the TV.

"Yes, she knows about that woman. Sounds like you knew too."

"I saw them kissing at the party. I didn't know what to do." My throat tightened.

I felt Tia Amelia's hand before I saw it.

"It's not your fault you didn't say anything."

I looked out the window where the biggest fluffiest flakes fell. Mom hated driving in the snow, and the Buick needed new wipers. And Mom moved like lightning when she was mad.

When we saw the headlights come up the driveway, Tia Amelia told me to rush upstairs. I wanted to see Mom and Dad, but Tia Amelia told me to give them some time. I sat next to my bedroom door to not miss a word.

"Where's Leonardo?"

"I told him not to come home." Mom sounded calm.

"Until?" The word extended at the end, like Tia Amelia wanted Mom to chime in before the whole word was done.

"I just told him not to come home."

And he didn't come home that night. There was no screech of the front door, or the pop of the fridge opening as Dad got his late-night snack. I crawled into bed, bringing the covers just under my chin.

Two Halves

Later that night, I woke up to the sounds of crying. I made my way quietly down the stairs, not turning on any lights. I didn't need to reach the bottom of the step to see into the living room. To see that this time it was Tia Amelia holding Mom. Mom on the couch, made of liquid foam. Mom's back folded over like a collapsed bridge. Mom whose face I couldn't see, buried in Tia Amelia who was rubbing her back. Tia Amelia whose eyes were closed, quietly rocking Mom back and forth, running her fingers in Mom's hair. Making the noises a mom does when there isn't anything to say, like she did to me when she told me Tio Bernardo and the twins died.

I had never seen my mom that way before. I wondered how she found out. I went back to my room. Questions of *why* and *what now* spun around. When the house went quiet, I tip-toed back downstairs. Tia Amelia was asleep on the couch. Mom was asleep in Dad's recliner.

The living room was dim except for the glare of the TV whose volume was so low, I only heard mumbles from the screen. It was an infomercial for *Secret Love*. This couple in sweaters sitting in front of the fireplace holding an album cover. *Now comes in three cassette tapes* scrolled down the screen. The lamp that was usually on over Dad's recliner was off. Mom used to leave that on when Dad was coming home late, so that he wouldn't bang his toe against the table in the dark.

Mom's face glowed red in the light of the TV. I wondered what she was dreaming about.

I decided to leave the TV on. It didn't feel right to leave them alone in the dark and I didn't want to turn on the lamp by the recliner because I knew Dad wasn't coming home. I covered Mom's feet a little more and went upstairs.

My room had one straight stripe from the moonlight running across it. It separated the room into almost two equal parts. When I got into bed, the light sawed me in half. Parts of me in different worlds.

Sanctuary

Dad didn't come home for the next couple nights. He did call me every day right before school to wish me a good day. I didn't ask him why he wasn't home, and he didn't talk about it either. We both knew why.

Mom did talk. She said Tia Amelia told her that I knew.

"I'm sorry I didn't tell you." I said. "I didn't know how."

"None of this is your fault, Itzel. I'm sorry you had to keep that to yourself. It must've been difficult." She put her hand on mine across the kitchen table. She wasn't crying at all like I saw her with Tia Amelia. Instead, her voice was steady.

When I learned that Dad was staying at the church, I went to go see him. Sanctuary is what I think they called it. It's what I learned in history class about the refugees. They sought sanctuary in churches because God's house was safe. Dad was some kind of refugee now, I guess. At least from Mom.

There was a mass letting out. A handful of old people swallowed by winter coats and oversized boots. They held closely to their purses, to their canes. One couple held on to one another as they walked down the aisle past me.

The candles flickered just enough for me to see each station under the stained-glass windows. Jesus on the ground covered in blood. Jesus on the ground with a heavy cross on his back, soldiers laughing instead of helping. A woman wiping Jesus's face.

I wasn't sure where exactly Dad was staying at in the church. All I knew is he was here somewhere. The empty church reminded me of the places in the vampire movies. The pews cold and the stained glass now just framed blobs. I stopped in front of the altar. It was covered in a white cloth. I knew Dad wasn't sleeping underneath it, but I saw him there anyway, like the homeless guys living in boxes that once held a fridge or a stove. I had never been in the church alone before.

"God," I said and it sounded weird. I don't think I had ever spoken to God out loud before. I turned around and still no one was around. The church was ten times bigger. The altar again seemed to shine on its own. A pure white. I looked up and there were paintings I had sort of paid attention to before. This time they moved like I was in a snow globe. God and Jesus there holding hands. Angels looking happy. None of them looked like me. God with his blondish hair and Jesus and his blue eyes. Father and son.

The Virgin Mary looked at them, separate, smiling. Fat little babies on clouds.

"I don't understand." I thought I had said it in my head, but I heard a soft echo around the altar. I didn't understand why Dad did what he did. Why was he living here now? When would Mom let him come home, if she ever did? Last week, I had my family. I knew who they were. Where they were. And now I didn't know what was going to happen. Was this the way it was going to be now?

"Itzel?"

I turned and saw Father Joe. He was wearing jeans and a shirt with the priest thing around his neck.

"It's very good to see you. Your Dad will be so happy." He smiled.

"Hi, Father." I did the sign of the cross because it felt like what I was supposed to do.

"I didn't mean to interrupt your prayer."

And I wanted to tell him that I wasn't praying. That I wasn't sure what I was doing, but it wasn't praying. That God wouldn't be listening to me, anyway.

"Follow me. Your Dad is staying in my office."

I followed him through the hallways of the house that was attached to the church. I had only seen the building from the outside. When I was little, I'd pictured the nuns and priests inside playing Scrabble using only holy words while drinking the church wine.

Father Joe knocked on his own office door and opened it. There was Dad sitting on the couch eating out of a Burger King bag. Fries hanging out of his mouth. His work boots side-by-side next to Father Joe's desk.

"Itzel came to see you," Father Joe said, and moved to the side so I could walk in. Dad ripped the rest of the fry off and put it back in the bag and wiped his hands on his pants. Father Joe closed the door behind me. His footsteps faded.

"Itzel," Dad said as he stood up.

I think he wanted to hug me, and I wanted him to, but I didn't move my feet, so he didn't either.

"How was school? Did Ms. Colvin give you that science test?" His voice was low and unsure. Dad was Dad and still not Dad at all.

"Why, Dad?"

"Nadine told me you knew. You knew since Friday." He sat back down on the couch and reached over to the desk next to his wallet and grabbed a box of cigarettes. When he lit it, he exhaled almost immediately.

I wondered if a hundred cigarettes would make enough smoke for him to disappear.

"I'm sorry, Itzel." I watched him rub his hands like he wanted his skin to fall off and still the cigarette managed not to burn him.

I heard footsteps above us and wondered if it was Father Joe or one of the nuns. The window started to tremble with the growing wind outside. That's when I noticed the mug there on the ledge. **#1 Priest** in bold black letters with the **T** in the shape of a cross.

"Father Joe let me use it," Dad said, finally looking at me.

I almost asked him what was in it. I decided it didn't matter.

"Why did you go with Nadine?" The words made their way towards the shelves and bounced off the bibles and the plastic bottles shaped like saints that were filled with holy water.

"Itzel..."

"How could you do that to Mom? How could you go with her?"

"Itzel. Stop."

"Did you want the opposite of Mom? Some blonde with blue eyes?"

"Stop Itzel! Stop!"

And everything stopped.

I sat on the floor near the door. Dad sat back down too. Soon the clock in the shape of a communion wafer said it had been ten minutes since the last time either Dad or I had said anything.

"I'm sorry, Itzel. I'm sorry I did that to you and your mom." He put his face in his hands and cried. He blended in with the blue couch.

The wind outside again rattled the windows. The Burger King bag was now wet with grease on the bottom. Dad hated cold fries.

I got up and sat next to him on the couch. I was still mad at him when he grabbed my hand with his wet fingers, saying *sorry, sorry, sorry* until the clock moved on to the next hour.

Spotlight

Her face was right there, front and center. Her cheekbones and her crooked eyebrows framed by neon blonde hair, and *Nadine* stitched in white on her uniform name patch the shape of an eye. *Employee of The Month* cut out in jagged block letters, lazily tacked below her picture. The corkboard was like the one in the grocery store where someone would pin a flyer of the lawnmower they were selling, or the Avon Lady would wallpaper it with her business cards. But on this corkboard, surrounding Nadine's face, were just notecards with various cursive in different inks that said, *Nadine! Thank you so much for being helpful!* and *Nadine! Your smile makes my day so much better!* and *Nadine! Thanks for delivering my baby during a snowstorm with one arm as the other was in a cast from saving a horse that had fallen over in the middle of the road.* The notecards seem to multiply the more I read them. By the looks of the board, I would've thought she was a good person and not the Cheater of the Month.

Dad told me that he'd pick me up at home and take me to dinner after work, but I knew that Mom didn't want to see him, so I told him I'd meet him at the factory instead. In the cafeteria, where I didn't have to wear safety glasses, but did have to be reminded that I'd seen him and Nadine kissing when they thought no one was around.

I didn't know if he was still seeing Nadine, or making out with her, or whatever he was doing that was gross. He told me he was still sleeping on a cot in Father Joe's office, but he didn't want me to visit him at the church after that first time. I thought maybe it was because he was embarrassed, but now I didn't know if maybe he was lying. Maybe he was living with Nadine in her apartment above a diner. Not that I knew where she lived. And come to think of it the only diner near us was Shirley's Diner on Lawrence that had nothing above it, just a huge sign with a coffee cup and a stack of neon pancakes. But still. Maybe he was already starting a new life with her. It had been a month. A month that had started with him trying to come over and talk to Mom, then him not coming over and calling Mom, which didn't work because I'd answer the phone and hold it up, and Mom would shout, "I have nothing to say!" After that, it was him giving me letters for Mom. I even saw Tia Amelia with a letter in her hands once, but once she saw Mom's face, she threw it in the trash with the others.

That week I kept thinking about last fall when I helped my neighbor Doña Teresa cook, and she had on a telenovela. In it, the women were all small-waisted, tiny-clothes-wearing, dark-haired, overly dramatic women, whose boobs were way too huge and on the verge of falling out of their bright dresses. Mom never allowed telenovelas in the house. I'm pretty sure she didn't think the sweet old lady next door with the gigantic stained-glass cross on her door did, either.

We were in the kitchen. Rosaries hanging off of each wall with tacks, and table vinyl placemats with bible passages, and a Jesus Christ magnet of just his head with a crown made of toothpicks and his eyes like the googly ones on those stickers they give you at school. Any time one of us opened the refrigerator door, the eyes would roll back and forth like miniature boomerang bowling balls till they stopped and looked down at the black-and-white photo of Doña Teresa back in '42 when she was just a teen in her prime. That's what she said, *I was a teen in my prime there*, and I didn't know what that meant, only that maybe I once prayed for me not to be a teen in my prime if it meant wearing my hair in rollers sitting on a stoop near a dog sprawled out that may or may not have been dead.

On top of a TV the size of a small house was a shrine to the Virgin of Guadalupe. There was a statue of the virgin surrounded by fake rose petals, and these miniature figurines of St. Francis and St. Anthony, and one random orange Hot Wheels car. And on the TV, the novelas. Women showing more skin than those at Montrose Beach. Women who kissed every man the color of Nestle Chocolate Quik and pretty much did *it* as much as they were allowed to show on TV, which on the Spanish channel was a lot.

Doña Teresa was in the kitchen but her head jolted to the TV every time she heard a slap, or a slam, or a moan. The tamale dough in her hand and her cross hanging down her narrow sagging boobs. Gray hair, and orange lipstick that was everywhere except her actual lips.

"You shouldn't be watching this, Itzel," she said. So I pretended to look away, or read the *National Geographic* that I brought with me, but really I watched the novela out of the corner of my eye so much it gave me a headache. Everyone seemed to cheat on each other in the show. Kissing and grabbing someone who wasn't their boyfriend or girlfriend, and then someone found out and slapped the other, followed by tons of yelling.

They spoke so quickly in Spanish that sometimes I didn't even understand them, but I don't think I was missing much. I don't think they were on TV for their words.

"Look at this filth," Doña Teresa said, but didn't change the channel.

Dark Match

Dad moved into his new studio apartment. The lease on the kitchen table said *Month-to-Month.* I wanted to ask Dad how many months he thought he'd be staying there, but I didn't. He was already annoyed that the stove wasn't working.

"Well, cold pizza never killed anybody," he said at last. He put the pizza on the table trays and we sat on the couch.

We didn't say anything to one another while we ate. The couch we were sitting on was also his bed. The kitchen was practically the headboard. I went to the bathroom and thought I was in an airplane one.

I wanted Dad to come home. It didn't feel right that he was there in that place. It was *cozy* like the ad said in the paper, and at least it was clean, but it wasn't home, even with the framed picture of me and him at the beach from last summer on top of the TV.

"How is it?" His chin pointed to the pizza.

"Good. I like it cold." And I meant it. I mean hot pizza is even better, but I like cold pizza too.

He nodded and went back to watching TV. I wondered what Mom was doing. This was my first overnight visit with Dad, and I don't think she'd ever had a night without both of us. I'd been hoping Tia Amelia would at least stay over with her, but she was on the night shift. Mom would be alone and I didn't know what that would look like. Would she cry? Would she play all those old cumbias that her and Dad would dance to? Would she look at old albums and drink wine and cry herself to sleep like that one woman did in that one movie?

"So, how's school going?"

"It's fine. I like English. Chemistry, not so much."

"Just like me. Your mom is more of a science genius." He laughed and then looked off to the window. That was my only favorite thing about the apartment. It overlooked a park, so we saw the top of the trees. Their leaves like shiny paper that covered those fancy chocolates.

Dad took a deep breath. "How's Fred?"

"He's fine," I closed my eyes for a minute and saw Fred there in his black jacket with the white stripes down the arm.

"That's good."

That was all I needed to get me thinking about Fred for the rest of the night. Not that I wasn't already thinking about him when I got to Dad's, but now I was thinking about him even more than before, like when you are playing red car and blue car and you couldn't stop seeing red cars. They were everywhere.

An hour later, Dad was sitting on one end of the couch snoring. I was watching a tape of *GLOW*. The television's light glared on and off on him like a broken spotlight. His belly looked bigger than before. His hair was longer than usual.

He'd bought a cot as thin as cardboard from Kmart so I'd have a place to sleep when I came over. I unfolded it and took the pillow and blanket I brought from home.

I left the television playing. Dad had tipped over and stayed asleep, so I covered him with a blanket that he had taken from home.

"Your dad is lucky your mom didn't burn his clothes," Fred had said at lunch that day.

"Why would she burn his clothes?"

"Cause she's mad. My mom said that's what some women do when their husband's cheat." He took a big bite of his sandwich.

Fred never made me mad. At that moment though, in the lunchroom filled with kids talking about video games and the latest movie, here was my best friend asking me if my mom burned my dad's clothes. I mean, we didn't even have a fireplace that worked, and no way was Mom going to go to the backyard and destroy her flowers. I didn't understand why Fred would ask me such a stupid question. It was almost like he had forgotten.

"Did your mom burn your dad's clothes when he left?"

Fred stopped midchew. He swallowed and then leaned in towards the middle of the table.

"What?"

"Did your mom burn your dad's clothes when he left? I mean, he left you guys. So did your mom burn his clothes?"

His face began to sag so much I thought it was going to fall onto his plate. I had never said anything bad about his father leaving.

He looked down at his sandwich but didn't touch it. His shoulders rose as he took a deep breath. Chairs squealed against the scratched pale-yellow tiles, and laughter choked the room. I knew I shouldn't have said it, but I didn't know why he'd brought up Dad leaving.

"Really?" he muttered as he got up from the table and walked away. He never looked at me. I watched him walk toward the door and toss his whole tray into the trash. The swaying doors didn't make a sound as he went through them.

The shadows on Dad's apartment's ceiling and walls were different from the ones at home. The trees from the park didn't cast shadows, but somehow there they were. Trees in the living room. Dark gray trees with leaves the size of dimes. I missed Mom. I missed Dad, even though he was an arm reach away. What I missed was them together in our house. Did Dad still think of it as his? I was starting to know that when Mom said *we*, it meant just her and me.

The only window in the apartment was open just enough for me to hear the people outside. I got up, making sure not to wake Dad as I walked past the TV. There was a black-and-white movie with a vampire. He had the thickest head of hair I'd ever seen.

I poked my head out the window as I heard voices again. Two floors below was a couple sitting on the stoop. The girl's hair was in a high ponytail. The boy wore a dark cap. They both had on white gym shoes.

"You're fucking crazy," the boy said. The bill of his cap turned toward her.

"I'm fucking crazy? I'm fucking crazy?" Her ponytail began to spin.

They muttered something I couldn't hear. A bus stopped and spit out a short woman with a huge purse and a man holding a brown paper bag. They went in opposite directions. Neither noticed the boy, the girl, or my head hanging out the window like one of those American flags rich people hang from the front of their big nice houses.

"I can't believe you, Rudy."

And even though I couldn't hear her or couldn't see her face, I knew she was crying.

Her back bent; her ponytail crept back into her head. Her white gym shoes were more scuffed than his.

Rudy uttered something I couldn't hear as he put his hand on her back. She shot away from it. Scooted over on the stoop. He shook his head. The bill trembled there in the night. His hands went back to his lap.

She stood up. Her hands on her waist. She looked straight ahead to the lavanderia, which was rather full for a late Saturday night. The 24-hour sign bordered in neon-white bubbles. She looked up at the sky. Her ponytail tilted back enough where I saw her forehead. Smooth and white like the middle of an ice cream sandwich. Then I saw her head tilt more back and I looked up to see what it was. There were stars upon stars above us, more than I'd ever seen, like pin points in black cloth. I wanted to wake up Dad and tell him because he told me once that he wanted to go to the moon. He wanted to float around in space surrounded by stars. I turned to look at him and there he was on the couch. Snoring as loud as the dryers across the street. He wasn't anywhere near the stars.

I poked my head back out and the girl was now looking down at the boy whose bill was still facing forward. Had she seen me looking up when she had? Had she tilted her head so far back that she could see my chin with the scar from when I fell back in first grade?

I couldn't hear them anymore. I only heard the dull scream of someone on TV. Dracula must have gotten someone. The girl walked away toward the dim street. The boy sat there. His bill only turned her way as she turned the corner.

I was sorry about what I said to Fred. For bringing up his dad that way, but I was still mad at him. Maybe I should've told him that hearing the words *cheat* and *husband,* as in my dad, wasn't right. Not from him. Not from my best friend, saying it in a way that didn't mean anything. Maybe on Monday, I'd tell him. Maybe on Monday I'd say I was sorry. Maybe on Monday, I'd tell him that I thought everyone had gone fucking crazy.

Dad woke me up with bacon and chocolate-chip pancakes. Cumbias were playing and the window was still open, the sun one bright square sliding down the wall onto the couch and floor.

"Sorry I fell asleep. You must've stayed up late. You didn't even wake up when I yelled, 'Fire!'" Dad laughed.

"Yeah. I was up watching a vampire movie." I hoped he wouldn't ask me which one, or what happened. He didn't.

We sat down to eat on the couch. Each of us again with our own table tray.

"A tray for one, madam," he said. He even did the whole towel-over-the-arm thing and bent down. I pretended to laugh. He was trying hard to keep me from asking about Nadine, or his apartment.

"Dad." I was going to tell him the pancakes were good. I was going to be nice even though he had gone and messed everything up. I looked from the crispy bacon and the thick pancakes to the table tray that was made to look like real wood, to the many cracks in the floors, to the small TV and car horns coming through the window, to the broken oven, to Dad who was trying so hard to make things normal, but they weren't normal and all I wanted was for us to be normal again. Why did he have to go with Nadine? Why did he kiss her? Why didn't he love us anymore? And then I didn't want his stupid pancakes and I didn't want to be in that crappy apartment, and I just wanted to go home, and I knew that meant he couldn't come.

I muttered the words.

"Did you say something?"

"I said, 'Are you fucking crazy?'"

The pockmarks on his cheeks turned into craters. His face sunk in and his eyes took over. He moved the table tray away from him fast, but not one drop of his orange juice made it out of the red plastic cup. He stood up. Bare feet, his jeans ripped at the bottom, the black t-shirt he wore with the factory logo on the chest. Nadine probably had the same shirt. He stood over me. I looked back at my plate.

"What did you say?"

The pancakes were undercooked in the middle. Some chocolate chips weren't melted at all. He was blocking the sun that had warmed my feet. I watched his feet. They didn't move, and I felt his eyes on the top of my head. I held onto my fork. I watched one foot take a step back.

"Look, Itzel, I know you are–" His voice didn't soften. He was mad. I remember Dad getting mad before. At Mom for driving without a license even though he was too sick to drive me to school. He yelled at her that time. He got mad at me for letting go of his hand when we were crossing the street. Spanked me right there on the sidewalk, yelling that I could've died.

"I said–" I moved my table tray away from me. My orange juice spilled onto my pancakes. I stood up and looked up at him. I thought I was going to dissolve right there. A puddle of myself drying in the sun. It wasn't fair. He had ruined everything. He had taken away our family, and for what? Some white woman who knew he had a wife and kid. Maybe if Mom was blonde. Maybe if Mom had blue eyes. Maybe Nadine made him feel more important because of it.

"I said–"

"Watch it, Itzel." He didn't move. I couldn't smell the bacon any more, or hear the birds chirping outside. This was it. This was going to end here. Whatever *this* was. Mom and him and Fred and this shitty apartment and going to church every Sunday praying for things that were never going to happen. I didn't know who this Dad was who cheated, or Mom who cried when she thought I was asleep and spoke about forgiveness until she actually had to forgive, or Father Joe who said cheating was a sin but prayed for Dad more than for us. I was tired. I didn't want to be Itzel anymore.

"Are you fucking crazy?"

Dad took a deep breath and the wind from the open window tightened around us.

I closed my eyes and started to cry. "Why did you mess everything up, Dad? What did we do wrong?" I fell on the couch, my ankle hitting the corner. And I cried there into my hands, afraid to look at him. "Just tell Mom you're sorry and you'll never do it again."

"I can't do that, Itzel."

"Why not?"

"It's complicated." He put on his shoes and reached over to give me mine. "C'mon. Your mom will be here soon."

"No." I moved away from him. "You have to tell me why you can't fix this."

"Nadine's going to have a baby."

And the room went still.

"Your mom knows, and that's why there is no fixing this. There is no me coming back home. I'm sorry."

I looked at him and said nothing. He sat back down and pulled the table tray towards him. The remote in his hand.

I heard the volume on the TV get louder before I grabbed my things and slammed the door behind me.

"What's wrong, baby?" I cried there in the car as Mom held me. I only stopped long enough for her to let go and drive us away.

Fred was on my front porch when we got home. I wiped my eyes with my jacket sleeves.

Mom spoke up as we pulled in. "Do you want me to tell him you don't feel well?"

"No, it's OK. Thanks."

We got out of the car. Mom carried my pillow and blanket.

"Hey Fred. Why don't you come inside? I'm going to make a late lunch." Mom walked inside before he even had a chance to answer.

"How was your dad's new place?"

"It was fine."

"I'm not sure what happened at school on Friday. I'm sorry if I said something that made you mad. I didn't mean to. I was just talking shit, I guess. I'm not even sure why I said that."

"I'm sorry too." I put my head on his shoulder.

"Your dad's wasn't fine, was it?"

I looked across the street to the *For Sale* sign on the neighbor's lawn. They had lived there for years. The little old couple were now too old to live on their own. That's what Mom told me. *Must be so sad. To make a home and then not to be able to live in it anymore.*

"No, it wasn't fine. It totally wasn't fine," I wanted to tell him everything that happened. About the shadows of the trees, and how my parents were supposed to grow old together like that old couple, and how I realized nothing would ever be the same again.

"Let's go inside. I'm hungry," I said instead. Before I opened the door, he turned me towards him. His hat pulled down over his ears. He was already getting so much taller than me.

"You know you're my best friend, right? Even when I knew you were mad at me. Even when I made you mad." And he hugged me. I did have my best friend. It felt like that was all I had to hold onto.

Sign Here

The divorce papers came on a Tuesday.

"Are you at least 18?" the messenger asked me. Some kid not that much older than me.

"Yes," I said, lowering my voice even though I knew girl's voices didn't get deeper the older they got.

He shrugged his shoulders and I signed on the dotted line.

Mom wouldn't be home for another two hours. I opened the manilla envelope and slid out a neat stack of paper. The header was like they have on those legal shows. I saw Mom's name vs Dad's name, and for a second it was like they were wrestling. I saw the announcer calling each of them from their corners and them going at it. Mom flipping Dad over. Nadine on the sidelines cheering Dad on, or maybe even waiting to get tapped in. I, there in the middle of the ring watching both destroy one another.

After the fight with Dad, he called me and asked me how my day at school was. *Good*, I said. *That's good*, he said. That was our daily phone call that week. Everything was good.

Good this and good that. None of it actually was good, though.

That Thursday's call he'd added something new: "I want to share custody with your mom, so she has you during the week and I every weekend. I'm trying to change my schedule so I can also pick you up from school a couple times a week. Sounds good to you?"

"That's fine."

And now there on paper were the words he'd spoken to me, but in the legal way. There it said *joint custody*. There it was official that we'd never be a family again. It was never going to happen and instead I would be *joint* until I was of legal age.

I tried to read through the rest. It was talking about child support and who would stay in the house. It said they were getting a divorce due to *irreconcilable differences* and I had to go find my dictionary to see what exactly that meant.

Irreconcilable differences - idiom
Inability to agree on most things, or on important things
Example: They are filing for divorce, citing irreconcilable differences.

They couldn't agree on a lot of things when they were together. What to name me. What house to buy. They couldn't agree on what was important to them, like each other. Like being a family for one. Maybe it was me. Maybe I was the reason.

On the last page, Dad had already signed it. He probably signed it there at his table tray next to his couch. The shadows of the trees watching. Or maybe he signed it over some fancy dinner with Nadine as she cheered and applauded like a circus walrus.

I put the stack neatly back into the folder and closed it. The flap didn't stick anymore and I knew Mom would know. It wasn't my business, really, but then again it was, and she wasn't hiding it from me anyway.

I went to the factory without telling anyone where I was going. The front desk lady knew who I was and told me Dad was working, but she would call him down.

"Oh, and is Nadine working today?"

The woman looked at me over the top of her huge glasses shaped like a framed bra on her face. "And what business do you have with Nadine?"

"She bought some Girl Scout cookies from me and I'm here to collect," I smirked. That twinkle-in-the-eye smirk like when I want extra candy before bed.

"She's off today. And aren't you supposed to take them to her house?"

"Oh. I lost the paper with her address. And I tried to look her up in the phone book, but I couldn't find a Nadine Smith."

"Smith? Her last name is Anderson." The phone rang and she answered, getting lost in whatever conversation had started on the other end.

Now I could find her in the phone book. I wanted to see where she lived. Where Dad was probably going to live soon.

I sat down in the lobby. The magazines were several years old. Folded corners or no corners at all.

"Itzel, everything OK?" There was Dad in his uniform. His eyes were wide open.

I stood. "Yeah, Dad. Everything is fine. I just wanted to say—" I saw the receptionist meet my eyes and then looked down as though she was writing something. Dad noticed, and led me into the hallway.

"What is it, Itzel?" He actually looked worried. Like he actually cared. I didn't even know why I went there in the first place. I didn't know what I wanted anymore. What I wanted wasn't ever going to happen.

"I saw the divorce papers."

He sighed. His hands in his pockets. He wasn't really looking at me at all. That's probably what he looked like when Mom first asked him about Nadine.

"Your mom shouldn't have—"

"I looked at them before she got home. Now, I know what joint custody really means. It means I will be split."

"Itzel. Let me take off work early and we can go talk." His eyes were red. I hadn't noticed before.

"No, it's OK." I thought about the child support the papers mentioned, and I didn't want him to get in trouble. "I just wanted to say that I'm still mad, but—" And then there was nothing.

"I know, Itzel. I'm sorry."

I walked out of the factory. I told Dad to stay even after he told me again that he would leave work early. "I'm going to go hang out with Fred," I told him, and that was true.

I knocked on Fred's door. He opened it. A pencil behind his ear like he was an old math professor.

"My turn. Let's go. We're going to go find Nadine."

2F

I knew why Mom was leaving Dad. I didn't know why Dad left Mom. I had seen Nadine those two times, but I didn't know any more about her. That was one topic that neither of them wanted to talk about, and one topic that I knew would make them both mad if I asked.

"Where's your phone book?" I asked as soon as I walked into Fred's living room.

"The yellow pages?"

"No, the white pages."

Fred left the living room. I heard him walk into the kitchen.

He was doing his homework on the living room table. A bottle of Coke next to his English Lit book. I didn't know when I was going to have time to do my homework. I had more important things to take care of.

"My mom uses it to prop open the basement door." He handed it to me. The cover was cold and glossy. It was heavy. All 1000+ pages of it. I started to look for Andersons, but there were so many, and the type was so minute I was getting a headache. I sat on the floor next to the living room table. Fred plopped right next to me.

"So, we're looking for your dad's girlfriend in there?" He peeked at the pages as I turned them. We hadn't kissed again since that first time. I wanted to, but it felt like it was always the wrong time. I turned the pages to A. There were way more Andersons than I thought. They almost took up a whole page by themselves. Carol. Joanne. Bea. I scanned the list so quickly I ended up at Andrews.

"There," Fred said and pointed.

"That has to be her," I said, and tore out the page like I had seen in the movies. I folded it up and put it in my coat pocket.

"Now what?"

I really didn't know. The address was two bus rides away. I knew Dad was still at work and I thought maybe she was too. I just wanted to see where she lived. Where maybe Dad went when he wasn't in his apartment.

"Let's just go take a look. I promise we'll be back before our moms get home from work."

"Alright then," Fred said and grabbed his jacket.

The Montrose bus was a couple of blocks away. Fred reached out and grabbed my hand. It made me think of the time when I told him about the affair. Only this time there was no running or crying and no question of whether he liked me. I felt weird when we passed the lady that ran the cleaners on the corner. She wore this oversized pink dress and her shoes were mismatched. More wrinkles on her face than the clothes she was steaming.

Her nose scrunched up when she saw us. Looked at us like we had said something bad about her kid or her dog, although maybe she didn't have either.

"Your mothers know what you two are doing?" she said as we passed her. Fred either ignored her or didn't hear. I turned to her. I wanted to say something and I almost pulled my hand away from Fred, but didn't. No, our mothers didn't know what we were doing. Holding hands on our way to check out my dad's mistress's living quarters.

"Don't listen to her," Fred said. "She's probably all alone."

I turned back when we crossed the street and she was gone. Maybe she was alone. Maybe seeing us hold hands gave her some kind of bad memories.

The bus was packed so we ended up standing. Some little kid was screaming that he wanted his crackers. Some guy kept yelling, *Really? This is ridiculous!* every time the bus stopped. I couldn't wait to get off the bus.

"You never liked crowds," Dad and Mom would tell me when parties got too packed or too many people were around. And I didn't. We never figured out why. Sometimes the why doesn't even matter anymore.

When we got off at Lincoln, I could breathe again.

"You OK?" Fred leaned his head right in front of my face.

"I'm OK now. It was just all those people." I watched the bus ride away and swore I still heard the screaming toddler through the closed windows.

I didn't think I could handle another crowded bus ride.

"Let's just walk there," I said. "It won't take us that much longer." I knew we had some time before our mothers got home and as long as we took both buses back, we should make it on time OK.

We didn't hold hands this time. Neither of us tried. Instead, we each had our hands in our jacket pockets. Mine felt the paper from the phone book.

"Maybe another twenty-minute walk?" I looked over at Fred and he was looking at the stores as we passed. He stopped at the one where they made suits. **Custom** in fat charcoal letters on the yellow sign.

"Do you think I'll ever have a suit like that?"

"Do you want a suit like that?" It was black on the headless mannequin. The tie was striped with blue and green.

"I don't know. I don't know if I'll ever need one. But maybe I'll need one like that one day."

The mannequin had the shiniest shoes I'd ever seen. They had this curved stitching on the side like a baseball.

"Maybe one day," Fred said and started walking away. I followed, catching a glimpse of the shoes one more time.

Goldblatt's was having a sale. RadioShack had posters as big as their windows. Cars went past us and so did some people. It was almost like walking on that escalator at the airport with the neon lights above. It seemed to never end. Maybe we should've taken the bus. Maybe Fred wasn't talking because he was tired of walking and thinking the same thing.

"Is this it?" Fred stopped and pointed to a window above a Chinese restaurant. I looked at the White Page.

"Yeah, that's it."

There were these apartments above the stores. The entrance was all glass, similar to Mancho's, although there were at least ten doorbells on the side. I searched for *Anderson*, but couldn't find it. The **Do Not Solicit** sticker on the sign was faded.

"Now what?" Fred said. He looked at the doorbells with me but couldn't see an *Anderson* either.

"What apartment is hers?"

"2F."

"There are only 3's on this side," Fred walked over to the glass door a few feet away. There were more bells. All starting with 2's.

Anderson was the fourth bell from the top. The name was printed on that black plastic that comes out of a machine. I had asked my parents for one for Christmas. The letters always white and raised.

"So, you going to ring it or what?" Fred seemed a little annoyed.

"What's wrong with you?" But I didn't make a move. A truck passed by and honked the horn. Made me jump a little. When I looked back Fred was rolling his eyes.

"What do you mean? All I asked you was whether you were going to ring the bell. Why you trying to pick a fight?"

"I'm not trying to pick a fight."

"Yes, you are."

"No, I'm not." And with that the front door opened. This guy holding a Pomeranian in the crook of his arm walked out.

"Excuse me," he said, and Fred and I parted to let him through. The little dog had a pink ribbon in its hair.

Fred held the door open for him but didn't let it go as the guy and his dog walked away.

"Well?"

I knew what he meant. Why ring the bell, when she could look out the window and see who was there? When it gave her time to think of the voice coming through the intercom. Why not just catch her by surprise?

We walked up the carpeted steps. Burgundy and new. The smell of spices filled the hallway. Fred behind me. The wooden rail slick under my sweaty palm. One of the doors on the first floor had a wreath on it. It was plastic for sure since it wasn't Christmas, but was a bright green. The *Welcome* in wooden letters painted red.

Walking the next flight of stairs shouldn't have seemed longer, but it did. Maybe my steps had slowed. Maybe the steps were bigger and grew more and more like that beanstalk in that one story Dad told me when I was little. The story where I kept asking why Jack wanted to go up in the first place. Why he didn't just stay on the ground where it was safe. *Cause curiosity is sometimes more rewarding,* Dad said. And now I understood what he meant. I wanted to climb and climb and see why her, and what was in that apartment.

The smell became stronger as the steps began to narrow. They turned to the second floor and there was a long hallway. The wallpaper covered in brown flowers that may have once been orange. I really couldn't tell and really didn't care. 2A was to my left. I turned to see Fred behind me. His head was hanging down as though he thought this was a bad idea, but wasn't going to say anything. I wondered if he didn't like me anymore. If this was the moment he was going to realize that I wasn't the girl he thought he liked.

"It's right there," Fred said.

I took a deep breath. I was going to knock, right? I was going to knock. I'd come this far. I was going to see if Dad already had some of his stuff there, and how she lived, and if she had nicer things than Mom.

"You don't need to knock," Fred said. He put his hand on my shoulder and then took it away just as fast.

"You knocked at Mancho's. You did it. You were scared, but you still did it," I took another deep breath as my hand went into a fist and I knocked on the door. I didn't know what I was going to say if Nadine or Dad opened the door.

I knocked again. I wasn't sure how long it had been from the first knock. Ten seconds. Ten minutes. My eyes stayed on the *2F*.

"No one is home, Itzel. Let's go." Fred wanted to say more. I could tell by the way the last word hung like a streamer.

"But—" and then there was nothing. I didn't know what I was going to do anyway if she did open the door.

"It's OK," Fred said and took my hand and this time I let him take it. He led me down the stairs and to the bus stop. Just like when I told him about Dad having an affair. He was in best-friend-saving mode, and I let him.

When we got back on the bus, I closed my eyes, feeling the bus hit potholes. What Dad and Mom called *swiss cheese streets*. The joke that they each laughed at when they were happy.

"Thank you," I said, and gave Fred a hug. He smiled and hugged me back, but didn't turn around when he walked into his house.

Mom wasn't home yet, so I left her a note on the table and went to bed. The sun was just starting to set, and orange glow filled my room in streaks like the pencil rays I had seen earlier.

My room was construction paper. Torn at the ends where the tape was coming apart.

I was dozing off when I heard Mom come home. She called my name and then must've seen the note because she didn't call me again.

Going to sleep. Sorry I opened this. That's what the note said. I'd left it on top of the divorce papers. There was a *why* in pencil that I'd erased, but not enough that she couldn't see it.

Baby Jesus

Some months later, Nadine had the baby.
This little baby like the Jesus everyone sees in
books and painted on murals. I didn't hate this
little baby, but I saw him just that once.
Nadine was there in the hospital room on the
bed and she smiled at me. I wasn't sure if it
was cause she was still high from all the drugs
or because now she had a real kid that was just
hers and Dad's. I said hello to her.

"Do you want to hold him?"

I sat in the chair next to her and she put
him in my arms. Here was this little tiny
meatloaf with blue gumballs for eyes and a
blonde fuzzy head and he was sleeping. So
quiet. And Dad was taking pictures. I heard the
click click click of him advancing the film and
each flash like an explosion. The nurse with
the patterned scrubs covered in tiny grilled-
cheese sandwiches opened and closed the
curtains like they were flapping wings. Nadine
was saying *aww* and I think she forgot at that
moment that she hated me or that I still hated
her for taking away my dad. Dad was all giddy.
Would he have smiled like that if the other

baby would've lived? The baby they still didn't know I knew about? Didn't Dad know that it was weird for him to bring his daughter to the hospital where his girlfriend just had a baby?

The baby started to feel heavy in my arms, but kept sleeping.

"Thomas...Thomas..."

I looked up and now Dad was sitting next to Nadine on the bed. He was caressing her hand. The one with a band-aid over it. And they said, "Thomas. His name is Thomas," and we didn't have any Thomases in the family, and that's when I knew. That's when it hit me that this wasn't my family. I was invited here, but when I left this room, I'd be going home. Dad had a new family. And I started to feel sick. My arms were wet and soaked with sludge and I couldn't move and yet at the same time I was floating away and away from them. I saw them from above, Dad and Nadine and Thomas all three there in the sunlight, the nurse finally leaving the curtains open so the sun could shine on them as though they were the new family. Cloaked in light and new beginnings.

"You alright?" Dad finally noticed me. I gave Thomas back to Nadine gently, so not to wake him. I hurried toward the door.

"Itzel?" Dad said.

"Leo," Nadine said.

I left the room and didn't look back.

I walked the thirty minutes home. I could've called Mom, but I just didn't want to talk to anyone. I felt alone though on every block there were kids playing and adults laughing and on the corner was a line to buy paletas as the ladies joked with the paletero.

When I got home, Mom was on the couch drinking her tea out of this mug I had never seen before.

"Itzel? Why didn't you call me? I would've picked you up." I'm not sure what she saw. What I looked like in that moment. But I stood there in the living room and I heard the mug plop onto the table and next thing she was holding me.

"Why, Mom?"

And for the first time since this all began, Mom cried in front of me. I felt her arms around me, and her tears rolling and rolling down upon me like a summer storm, and she said, "I don't know, baby. I don't know."

Ticket For One

I dreamt that night that I was lost. I was on a roller coaster that slithered along the beach, and the only seat taken was mine. I heard the hissing of the coaster, and the sand sprayed upward as it rolled. Fred was in the water, bouncing with the waves, smiling and waving. His arm seemed so long. He didn't say a word, but I knew he wanted me to join him.

The sky was night except for where a star had been cut out, like a gigantic cookie cutter had been pushed into the sky and then removed. There was nothing in that star, just blackness, the rest of the sky dark glittering with lights.

Petals of tulips the size of my hands began to fall from the sky and floated on top of the water. And as much as I wanted to catch one, when they landed on me, they melted almost immediately.

I sat in the back, sliding back and forth along the wooden seat, and when I looked ahead, I saw my father in the front seat alone, but facing me; his back turned to the front of the coaster, turned away from the sand ahead.

I wanted to go to him. He didn't look happy or sad. He was as lost as me, as though he didn't know just why he was there, or who he was. He slid back and forth, but didn't try to hold on or stop himself from crashing into the sides. I heard the bruises forming on his arms and his legs with each jerk of the train.

The coaster slowed and finally I noticed under the glowing moon the paintings on the inside of my seat. They were cups of coffee with stems coming out of them like straws, covered in thorns, but with no flowers.

I ran my finger over one and it sliced my finger. Blood dripped onto the floor. I turned to the ocean and saw my mom there. Just her eyes and her forehead and the tip of her head, as everything else was underwater. How could she breathe? Wasn't the water filling her lungs? How could I still hear her call for me and my father with her mouth engulfed in waves?

The coaster slowed and then the many seats between Dad and me disappeared. He looked at my mom. The bottom of her eyes were touching the ocean, her tears floating, glowing on the water. Dad went to say something, but nothing escaped. I reached out my hand, not so I could help him, but so he could bring me to him.

He didn't take my hand. Instead, he kept watching my mother with thousands of her floating glowing tears surrounding her, stuck on her face and head like leeches. I couldn't see her eyes anymore.

Lost & Found

"I know you're upset with me, but you need to listen to me," Dad said when I picked up the phone. I listened.

"I need to tell you a story," he went on. "When you were just four or five, we went to the library. The big main one downtown. Four floors. The children's library was on the second floor, and your mom said she had to go to the bathroom, so I should watch you. *Of course*, I said. Two seconds after she walked away, I turned to see the books you were looking at scattered on the floor, but I didn't see you.

Excuse me, I said to this lady that was there with her kid. *Did you see a little girl?* And she shook her head and went back to reading to her baby. *Itzel! Itzel!* I started to worry because I was walking up and down these aisles and started to think how you loved to climb and all I needed was for you to climb up one of the bookcases and them all falling on you and crushing you. I had never been so frightened. Then I started to think what if someone took you? You were so small and light. *Itzel! Itzel!* I started to yell louder and louder, and people started to look at me, but no one offered to help.

Finally I turned and saw you at the end of an aisle. You were so into a book about lions. One where you can feel the hair. And you laughed. *Papa. Look! Look!* and I bent and cried there. I cried while you wiped my face and told me not to be sad anymore.

Your mom knew what happened. She never asked me, but she saw my face when she came back. I never cried. She knows me better than anyone and knew what would be the thing to break my heart. I promised to never lose you again.

I know things are drastically different now and I want you to know I didn't plan any of this. And I'm disappointed to say that I didn't think of the consequences. But it all happened and I can't take it back, no matter how much I wish I could."

I held the phone too tightly to my ear and it burned. The cord wrapped tightly around my arm. He was living with Nadine now. In that apartment with the ugly wallpaper that led to the door that read 2F. I refused to go inside. I'd meet Dad outside, or he'd pick me up and we'd have dinner, just us two. But I saw him there at that moment, holding the phone, in some new leather chair that looked nothing like his old recliner, maybe holding a frame of us when he took me to the zoo. The picture where we were making faces and wearing animal hats. He took it when he left.

"I don't want to lose you again."

Everything is Temporary

The house was still, except for the muffled rumbling of the ice maker downstairs. If I really listened, I was sure I could hear the clasp of the suitcase hidden in Mom's closet. I wondered if I snuck back into her room like I had before, what would be in the suitcase now? Maybe it was emptier. Or maybe the divorce papers were in there, on top of all the other documents that marked life changes. Maybe now when it was opened, there was a cardboard cutout that popped up like one of those fancy Hallmark cards, with Mom and me on one side and Dad on the other.

I thought of Abuela and the buried note Abuelo left for her. Was it even still there? Had the rain that day washed away the words? Did they float within the ground until ants carried them away to their homes?

Mom's *Are you OK?* followed by a kiss on my forehead when I hung up the phone with Dad. Us listening to music while we made tamales. Singing along to songs we once sang as a trio.

I got up quietly so I wouldn't wake up Mom. Made my way downstairs, making sure not to step on the one step that shrieked. Everything was covered in darkness except for the *11:17* that shone from the clock in the living room. Seconds not shown but still ticking by.

I went over to the phone. Letting the cord fall freely. I dialed.

"Hey, Dad. Can you talk?"

Acknowledgments

Writing this book was like embarking on a thrilling adventure, complete with unexpected twists, daunting obstacles, and moments of pure magic. Along the way, I was fortunate to have the support and encouragement of some incredibly exceptional people:

First and foremost, I want to express my deepest gratitude to my husband and daughter, Cesar and Viviana Vargas, for their unyielding belief in me. Their unwavering support kept me motivated during the challenging moments of writing. They provided me with snacks, hugs, and much-needed kicks in the ass when I needed them most. Their boundless love and confidence in my talent allowed my creativity to flourish. ooxxooXoXXx

I extend my utmost appreciation to my editor and publisher, Gerald Brennan of Tortoise Books, for taking a chance on this tale and believing in its potential. Your support and enthusiasm have meant the world to me, and I'm incredibly grateful for the opportunity to share my story with the world.

A heartfelt thanks to these distinguished authors, Eric Charles May, Patricia Ann McNair, Sahar Mustafah, Rob Rufus, Chris L. Terry, and Jeff Zentner, for graciously providing their time and offering such generous praise. Your kind words mean the world, coming from such esteemed and talented writers.

A huge shoutout to awesome fellow writers, Chris Maul Rice, Howard Simmons, and Edward Thomas-Herrera, who read my manuscript in its early stages and provided invaluable feedback. I am sincerely thankful for your time, your honesty, and your constant support throughout this journey.

I am profoundly thankful for my family— Rolando Alarcon, Doris Cole, and Megan Schildgen—and friends Erin Christian, Jennifer Jackson, and Don Woolf. Their steadfast belief and boundless enthusiasm in me have been a constant source of encouragement and motivation. Your faith in my abilities has propelled me forward, even when self-doubt threatened to hold me back. Thank you for standing by me and cheering me on every step of the way.

I extend my gratitude to *Allium* and *Thalia Magazine* for featuring excerpts of this book. Special thanks to the Holland Prize for Fiction for recognizing it as a semi-finalist and to the Chicago Writers Association for awarding it an

Honorable Mention in the First Chapter Contest. Your support has been integral in bringing this book to fruition.

Lastly, to the readers who will embark on this journey with me, thank you for your enthusiasm and curiosity. It is my sincere hope that this book will resonate with you and perhaps even make a small difference in your lives.

Thank you, from the bottom of my heart.

— Cyn Vargas

ABOUT THE AUTHOR

Cyn Vargas, an accomplished author, has garnered acclaim for her collection *On The Way*, earning praise from *Shelf Awareness*, *Library Journal*, and more. Recognized as one of Book Scrolling's Best Short Story Collections, her work is celebrated by the *Chicago Book Review* and the Chicago Writers Association. Vargas's writing graces esteemed literary magazines like *Split Lip* and *Word Riot*, and made her a Top 25 Finalist in *Glimmer Train*'s Short Story Award for New Writers. Her piece was even chosen as a Symphony Space Selected Short, performed live and released as a podcast. She embraces her first-generation American heritage with pride, hailing from El Salvadoran and Guatemalan roots.

Find her at cynvargas.com

ABOUT TORTOISE BOOKS

Slow and steady wins in the end, even in publishing. Tortoise Books is dedicated to finding and promoting quality authors who haven't yet found a niche in the marketplace— writers producing memorable and engaging works that will stand the test of time.

Learn more at www.tortoisebooks.com or follow us on Twitter: @TortoiseBooks.

Printed in the USA
CPSIA information can be obtained
at www.ICGtesting.com
JSHW020137110624
64547JS00019BA/121